THE LAST BEEKEEPER

PABLO CARTAYA

ILLUSTRATIONS BY CARLOS VÉLEZ AGUILERA

An Imprint of HarperCollinsPublishers

*To my children, and all the world's children—I hope we leave
you a planet that shows we did our part, even, at times,
in spite of ourselves*

Beyond a doubt truth bears the same relation
to falsehood as light to darkness.

—LEONARDO DA VINCI

The environment is where we all meet, where we all
have a mutual interest; it is the one thing all of us share.

—LADY BIRD JOHNSON

CHAPTER 1

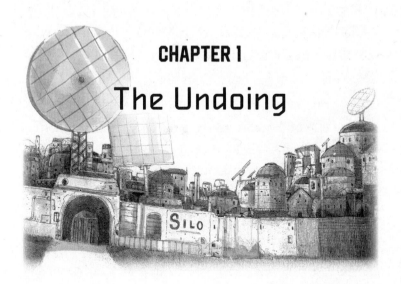

The Undoing

Most people come to Silo without noticing the carved marks on the lower section of its largest tower. Except me. I always look for the scratches on the cylindrical steel structure whenever we come to town. Nothing seems to take them away—not the tormentas that sweep through the Valley in the winter. Or the blistering calor that burns metal on the hottest days. Not the storms of polvo and lluvia and hail that come sporadic and brutal across the Valley. Nothing seems to remove them from my sight line—like they refuse to be fully forgotten. A reminder. A memory I want to forget but can't. I wish there was a way to make them disappear. To erase them forever.

Every time I see the marks, I see how little is left of the world I once had. A time when Mamá y Papá were with me. When fresas looked like actual strawberries instead of white marbles. I was little. Only six.

Six years later and I still can't wipe out the memory. I'm like one of those newer-generation V-probes. Smarter. Faster. But still carrying around some physical reminders of an older model. That's funny. I hadn't thought about myself that way before.

"Come on," Cami says, walking through the Town Welcome Center.

The last time my sister and I came to Silo, we barely had enough of a harvest to sell one full crate of strawberries. Now we have more, but they look worse than ever before. Our rows of fields grow only tiny, pale fruit bulbs. The drones just don't pollinate like they're supposed to, but that's probably because we haven't gotten upgrades in over two years. That's like an eternity.

The closed metallic garage gates buzz while our V-probes are scanned. On top of the gate there are two large solar panels. They're linked to smaller ones excavated over the years and reassembled along the walls that make up Silo—the most connected and technologically advanced town in the Valley.

The largest of the panels—a giant solar dish—powers the three silos that keep the Valley online. The reflected sunlight creates pulses of light that transmit signals to the photoelectric cells that give energy to miles of fiber-optic cables coiled inside the silo towers. They're the only towers in operation. There are a few older silos scattered across the Valley like lifeless monuments. Useless relics of failed connectivity.

The only ones that work are the ones beaming from Silo. The sun blasts on the panels all day. Even in the cold. There's no way we'll ever run out of power again. We won't ever have to be offline.

Right before sunset, the glare from the steel towers can be seen for hundreds of miles. Mayor Blackburn says it's a beacon. A reminder that the town of Silo is always there when the night falls and the cold sets in across the Valley. When hungry nightcats scavenge the countryside. When people stay inside.

Five motion cameras mounted across the garage gate blink and send a signal to our devices. Both of our V-probes ring. I look at my screen and see the Silo welcome penguin greeting us as we wait to be let into town. Silo's online System is big on extinct-animal avatars. It assigned me a panda with my username. I'm not big on pandas. *Any* animals really. They smell and they're dangerous and unpredictable. I can't change it though. The System's fire wall won't let me.

My V-probe earpiece vibrates, and Silo's overly cheery

concierge waddles on my screen and hums in my ear.

Camila Cicerón and Yolanda Cicerón of Lot 2506.

¡Hola! Proceed to your stand, and have a productive
day in Silo!

The little penguin's eyes flash green, signaling the garage gates to open. My sister and I walk under the massive Town Welcome Sign.

"¿Qué haces?" she asks.

I look up from my V-probe and see Cami staring at my screen.

"Just browsing TIE classes," I answer, really looking forward to my Advanced Neurolink class.

"Yoly," Cami says like she's annoyed. "Maybe you should take a break from school this quarter. I could use your help around la finca."

"What are you talking about?" I shoot back. "I've been waiting to take this class for over a year, Cami."

My sister tries to get my attention, but I'm still scanning for my neurolink class.

"I know, but we could put a pause on classes for a couple of months. It wouldn't be the end of the world. We'll sell some fresas, then get you logged back into the tech institution education—"

"Technologically Intuitive Education, Cami," I interrupt. "If you can't remember the name, just call it

TIE like everyone else."

My sister nods and I shake my head. She's so behind on upgraded technology. Cami is twelve years older than me, but she acts like she's fifty years older sometimes. Fifty years ago, *nobody* was online. There was no power anywhere. A whole generation born into darkness.

When I was born, the System had already been online for ten years. Now it's growing, with more and more applications and mods popping up every day. Mayor Blackburn says my generation will usher in the next technological revolution in human history, and I've got to make sure I'm a part of it. I look back at the TIE application and am just about to click on it, but Cami always has to get the last word.

"Life's not all tech and upgrades, Yoly. There are other things to think about as well."

I swear she turns on her Cami-es-Mamá mode *all the time*. Why can't she just be my sister for once? I'm not a child anymore.

Cami moves into town, shaking her head. I don't know what her problem is. She's been in such a bad mood lately.

I look back at the Welcome Sign, then at the three towers lining up like giant metal guards outside town. The System literally brought us back from the age of darkness. My sister should be more grateful.

"Just put the device down and help me set up our stand," she says without turning around.

I watch as Cami unloads the crate onto a long metal table. I'm about to put my V-probe away to go help her when it buzzes.

ARE122107: ¡Oye! ¿Qué pasa calabaza?

Cami huffs and shuffles her feet, then gives me a *look*. I know she's about to tell me to pick up a crate or something, but I can't ignore my best friend when she's pinging me!

Arelis always calls me "pumpkin" or some other kind of food that people used to eat when she messages me. Her birth month is December, so she has the number twelve after her name. My birth month is January, so my number starts with a zero and a one.

We've been friends ever since we started classes six years ago. She lost her parents a couple of years before mine, and we bonded over having annoying older siblings who act like our parents. She and her brother, Cornelius, live in a small house in the Outer Valley near the High Mountains. Way too far to walk, and SDVs are expensive.

I ping her back:

YOLA012108: ¿Qué pasa, amiga? Did you register for Advanced Neurolink yet?

ARE122107: No. Having trouble logging in. ¿Tú?

YOLA012108: Not yet. The System keeps sending me reminders, but Cami keeps telling me to wait. Ugh!

She's sooooo pesada sometimes.

Arelis sends an image of a hippopotamus spitting water while it laughs uncontrollably. Nobody's seen a hippo in like sixty years. Not that I would want to see one even if I could. They're kind of gross. And I read they were really mean and aggressive. Cami slams a crate in front of me and stares. I look at her, then back at Arelis's hippo image, and burst out laughing.

"What's so funny?" Cami asks.

"You look like a hippo with the face you just made," I tell her, still laughing.

"You're hilarious," she says dryly. "Can you please put that thing down and help me?"

Arelis pings back:

ARE122107: You heading to Silo?

YOLAO12108: Here now. We're setting up our stand at the market. Let's see if we actually *sell* any straw-berries this time.

ARE122107: I wish I got to spend time with my brother selling stuff. He's always rushing around. Never lets me go anywhere with him. At least he's letting me help him with this one thing.

YOLAO12108: What is it?

Arelis takes a minute to respond. I look at my V-probe's stats to see if I've lost connection, but I'm not surprised to see that everything's normal. Silo is the only place in

the Valley with full connectivity. It must be coming from
Arelis's end.

ARE122107: Hey, sorry about that. Anyway, it's cool
you and Cami farm together.

YOLA012108: Farming is the worst! Like a bleh to the
max. I would love to work in tech all day. Nature is def
not my thing.

My sister interrupts my conversation again by putting
a little box of pale strawberries in my face. I shove it away
and stare.

"Yoly, please put the device away. *Now.*"

My face must show how I feel because when I look up
again, Cami is staring at me with that irritating look she
gives when she's losing her patience.

"Please chill with the eye roll, okay?" she says, watching me. "Or I'll log you off the System."

"Yeah right," I snap. "You don't have the authority.
Besides, the System doesn't care whether we sell some
dumb strawberries or not."

Just because she's my "guardian" doesn't mean she can
just boss me around and tell me what to do whenever she
wants. Sorry con excuse me, but nah. No way.

YOLA012108: Ugh. Cami's acting like she's my mom
again. Chat later. Lemme know your class sched the
second you register!

ARE122107: ¡Bueno! Hasta luego, caramelo.

Arelis's polar bear avatar blows a giant kiss, which is kind of cute. Kind of.

I'm about to put my V-probe back in my pocket when my screen buzzes and I see my school emblem flashing. It's like it knew Arelis and I were waiting to register!

"Yoly," my sister suddenly blurts out. "¡No has ayudado con *nada*! You've literally been staring at your screen all day like a mindless drone."

My V-probe flashes, and I see the school door open on my screen, telling me it's time to pick my class for the semester.

"Well, this *mindless drone* is going to be a certified neurolink surgeon someday and make some real money," I snap back. "I just need to take one more class, and then I'll qualify for an apprenticeship. Bye-bye, fresas, *forever.*"

I wave at a sad little strawberry, then scroll and click along the virtual school halls. I find Advanced Neurolink and add it to my cart. I click on the bag icon and start the checkout process. Arelis must be logging in this very second. I want to see our avatars pop up in class at the exact same time. I swipe the icon to pay and see a huge sign shooting across my screen:

REGISTRATION DENIED—INSUFFICIENT FUNDS

"Cami, it's denying access! I think something went wrong with the credit transfer to the System."

Cami's face changes. Like the stress of the whole world

is landing on the dark circles around her eyes. I press her for answers.

"You didn't transfer the money, did you?"

I pace around the small space in our stand, waiting for my sister to explain. Finally, I slam my hand down and demand she answer me.

"Cami, say something! You know how important this is to me. Why aren't you helping me?!"

"¡Basta!" Cami yells out. I look around and notice a few people staring. The cameras posted on the lamps along Main Street train on our stand. Cami yelled so loudly, it made the System pay attention. "All you've done is stare at your V-probe all morning. You haven't helped unload *una* fresa. ¡Ni una! And now you're telling me *I* am not helping *you*? If you would spend a little time off your screen and more on what needs to be done in order to *pay* for your screen time, then maybe we would be in a better position to afford things like your TIE classes."

I don't say anything. Cami doesn't usually go off on me like that. Like, she nags me to do stuff all the time, but she rarely ever yells. This isn't some simple credit-transfer error with the Exchange. Something is wrong.

I log off of the school site and put my V-probe in my pants pocket. People go about their business again. The cameras adjust back to monitoring Main Street, and I'm left in the quiet wake of my sister's outburst.

"Are we okay with money?" I ask, softening my tone.

"No." Cami sighs, then tries her best to organize the pinkest-looking strawberries in the front for display. There aren't many. She digs into her jacket and pulls out a protein bar, taking a bite, then gulping a sip of water from her lapel.

She found the jacket at her Retreat, seven years ago. It has more functions than any wearable tech around. Tiny nanocams that can be activated to make the jacket look invisible. Deep inside pockets to hide stuff. It even makes its own water.

I keep looking at the coat. It's the most advanced tech we own. Maybe she can sell her jacket? We'd probably get a lot for it. We could use some of the profits to pay for school if there's any left over. As if reading my thoughts, Cami jumps in and crushes the idea.

"Hundreds of these jackets are brought to the repurposing labs every week," she says. "They get disassembled, and the microchips and tech are used for other things. And then the jackets get burned."

She points to a building down Main Street with a large chimney blowing smoke from the roof.

"There's no use for the fabric," she says. "Only the tech and metal pieces."

"Then how come you got to keep the jacket?"

"It's a reminder."

"Of what?"

Cami watches me for a moment, then moves to the front table to wait for customers. Silence fills our stand as the noise from the street picks up with more people visiting the market.

I remember seeing my sister—dusty jacket, hair in tangles, boots muddy and worn—walking up the front porch steps. Her left hand was shiny and spindly—an augmented prosthesis I noticed immediately. I hardly had time to ask her about it because she marched in and told me the worst news any kid could ever hear.

"Mamá y Papá are gone. Exiled," my sister said, moving into our house. "They're not coming back."

Nobody can survive outside the Valley. There's no power out there. Nothing to keep you from freezing to death within days. Exile is the worst punishment anyone can receive.

The rest of that day is hazy. Scattered memories. My sister gave no further explanations. Never shared what my parents could have possibly done to receive such a punishment. All she told me was to not be late to log in to school.

"They kick you out if you don't log in on time," she

said, then disappeared into her room.

That was the last time Cami talked about our parents. For six years, all she's told me to do is go to school, help around the house, and *don't* talk about what happened. I know it's because Cami finds the past too difficult to remember, but sometimes I can't help but think there's something more. Another reason why she doesn't like talking about our parents.

I look at my sister. She's busy lining up the little white-and-pink strawberries for display. She hands me an empty crate. I take it and stare at it for a moment. Technology is used to help us. We program it. We control what it does. Not like nature, which produces whenever it wants. Once I finish my last TIE class and an apprenticeship, I'll be able to get my neurolink medical certificate. Then I can rely on my training to make a living, enough for both Cami and me. No more counting on nature to produce some crops so we can live. Advanced Neurolink is my way out of farm life. I have to find a way to pay for school.

CHAPTER 2

The Exchange

A lady with a gigantic pheasant on her head stops by our booth. I've never seen anyone wearing an extinct animal as a hat before.

"Customer," Cami says, getting my attention.

"Where did you get the bird hat?" I ask the lady, who is looking across the street and ignoring our stand, even though she's standing right next to us.

"Yes, I see it," the lady says, still ignoring me. "I'm making reservations with the place now. Hola, sí, cuatro sillas afuera esta noche, por favor. I asked for a table outside. Yes, they're doing outdoor seating now! I know! It just keeps getting better and better. Just sent my data preferences over. I know. I just found an early twenty-first-century tea set. So rare! Do you see it? Look at the rounded glass. And this little thing that pushes down. They really did make magnificent things back then."

It's like she's talking to five different people all at once.

"Excuse me?" I ask again, but she doesn't pay attention. The pheasant's lifeless eyes stare at me, and I have to admit, it's kind of terrifying. I seriously don't know what I would do if that thing was alive, flapping around with those huge wings. No thank you.

The lady finally turns around to face our booth.

"These are not ripe," she says, then walks off like we don't exist.

Cami rearranges the strawberries to put the more pinkish ones in front again.

"She's wearing a neurolink," I say, pointing to the square device implanted on the back of the lady's head. "Those are worth a ton of money! She probably lives in the Remembrance district."

"Wealth doesn't buy manners," Cami says, moving a few white strawberries around. "Or taste. Who wears an extinct bird on their head like a hat? It's not even fashionable."

"Says the person who wears the same pair of boots, pants, and jacket every day of her life?"

Cami looks up and stares. "Do you realize how awful it is to flaunt an extinct animal as a fashion statement? Seventy percent of the earth's animal and plant population died in the last fifty years, Yoly. Didn't you learn that in school?"

I shift around anxiously and scoop out my V-probe. The school icon flashes. **DENIED** scrolls across my screen again.

Cami notices.

"I'm sorry," she says. "I didn't mean to bring up school."

"I have to get in before midnight, Cami. What if we sell some things from the old shed behind the house? Didn't Abuelita keep some stuff in there? There's gotta be something in that dusty shack we can use."

"Shush," she says, drawing close. "Don't talk about that."

"Why not? What's the big deal? It's just a shed."

"Yoly, please. Just . . . not here. We'll think of something, okay?" she says in her most assuring voice possible.

I examine her face and try to understand why she doesn't tell me anything. I probably never would have found out that we were having money problems if it hadn't been for my TIE class. Cami tries to avoid my gaze, but I scan her as she moves around our stand making herself busy.

My sister and I look alike. We're the same height, and

our features are practically identical. Dark eyebrows that fold into dark circles around our eyes. Mamá used to say we inherited our abuela's features. Like history copied the same face in between generations. My sister and I don't smile much, but our teeth are like mirrors of each other. My left front tooth overlaps my right. Cami's is the opposite. Right over left. Both a split screen of crooked.

If we were the same age, we could be twins. The only difference is our hair. Mine is a dark cloud, and hers is nothing but scalp. It was shaved when she went on Retreat years ago. She never grew it back.

Cami moves to organize the strawberries for the tenth time. It's like she knows I am still thinking about the shed because she turns to me and whispers.

"We can't talk about Abuelita, okay? Just trust me."

My head tries to map out an explanation but comes up with nothing. Why can't we talk about Abuelita and some old shed she used to work in? I haven't been in there in years. From what I remember, there was nothing but a desk and some machinery that didn't work anymore. The metal could be sold though. We could trade it in for money. Before I can press my sister, she turns and waves at Ms. Méndez in her orange stand across the street.

I can tell by the way Cami avoids eye contact that she's done talking about this. It's been like that forever. She still treats me like I'm four. No explanations. Just do what she says.

"I'm going to get a snack from the Tanakas' stand," I say, already bored standing in our lot and tired of trying to get an answer out of her. "You want something?"

"Yoly, we've barely been here ten minutes. Have a protein bar."

"They taste like grass and bits of rock, Cami. It's gross. The Tanakas might have licorice."

"How are they going to have licorice if they didn't have a sugarcane yield last harvest?"

"Unlike you, *I* think positive, Cami," I say. "Like, maybe they saved some?"

Cami mutters something about me being lazy under her breath. Ugh, she can be so pesada! Like, beyond annoying.

I decide to walk past the Tanaka stand for now and toward the center of town. The more time away from Cami, the better. She never wants to talk to me about anything. She doesn't talk about Mamá y Papá. She won't talk about money. She hardly even says anything about herself or her time on Retreat. It's like she operates in the private network of her own mind without letting anybody, not even her own sister, have the access code to connect.

I don't remember much about her when we were all home together. The four of us as one family. There are a few things, I guess. Like her laugh. She had the loudest laugh. It almost sounded like a nightcat—like the ones that prowl around the Valley.

Mamá would crack up hearing my sister's deep voice breaking into high-pitched hisses and low guttural growls. Then Papá would join in, and he and Cami would both take turns to see who could laugh with the deeper voice.

I approach Main Street and Remembrance Road. The mayor's mansion comes into view. It has a giant mirrored window that takes up two stories. One side of the house has a marble-and-concrete wall the length of a town block. The back of the house has a conveyor belt bolted onto a steel-doored garage and is connected to a back alley. The whole building looks like a metallic creature got bitten in half by the door.

The whole street has upgraded structures scrapped from the Dead City. Materials like wood and glass are mostly set up along Remembrance Road. Only people who make a lot of money live in the Remembrance district. People who have tech-based jobs like programmers, engineers, and surgeons. Like a neurolink surgeon—the best job ever.

A kid named Federico in my Systems Tech class lives around here. We've never met in real life, but I know he's from here. In class, he was always posting how his mom is lead engineer for the Westward System Expansion.

The WSE is a huge project to connect Silo to people who live in the Outer Valley. They're laying down fiber-optic cables for more reliable connectivity. That's why the silos around the Valley stand empty and decrepit—old and fading like the one on the Tanakas' farm. They were always breaking down and too far out of Silo to fix regularly, so they became obsolete in favor of a better plan. Because of the WSE, people like Cornelius and Arelis will be able to finally get full, uninterrupted access to the System.

Everyone knows the WSE is one of the most important projects in the entire Valley.

Federico was always strutting around in his galactic emperor avatar skin like he owned the universe. He liked Arelis and tried to connect with her in the System, but she shot him down like twenty times. Then he invited me to a virtual hang after Arelis had already said no! I can't stand entitled tech brats.

A door opens and Mayor Blackburn steps out. He's tall and has a full head of black hair. I'm always surprised by that fact. He's been in the Valley almost as long as Abuelita had been. A woman I don't recognize is with Mayor Blackburn. She hands him a jar of something amber colored.

"It's the last bottle," she says angrily.

"I know," he says. "I've been searching—"

"Search harder," she scolds. "We need to find it."

I step on a metal plank, and the screech echoes down the alleyway. Mayor Blackburn sees me. I turn and dart away but not before he calls out.

"Yolanda Cicerón, is that you?"

I stop in my tracks but don't turn around, even though I know he's already spotted me.

"It's nice to see you," he says cheerfully.

"Oh," I say, startled and also kind of embarrassed I was just standing outside his house like a total weirdo. The lady looks at me funny. The bottle goes into her coat, and she glares at Mayor Blackburn before going back inside.

"Sorry, Mr. Mayor. I was . . . I was just walking and, um, yeah. Well, bye."

I start off, hoping I don't have to speak to him. Talking to adults in real life is strange. My sister is technically an adult, but I don't consider her one—even though she insists she's so much older.

"Going back to market?"

"Um, yes, sir."

"I'll walk with you," he says.

"Oh, okay."

I amble down the dirt road and kick up dust as I walk. As we leave Remembrance Road, I take in the refashioned two-story buildings made from scrap metal salvaged from across the Valley and beyond.

Mayor Blackburn notices me looking.

"When the System powered up self-driving vehicles again, more and more materials from destroyed buildings were brought to Silo," he continues in a melodic story-teller voice. "We salvaged brick walls, steel doors blasted from fallen skyscrapers, large windows," he says, pointing to the structures all around us. "Anything that survived from the past was salvaged and brought to Silo. Repurposed as buildings for stores, apartments, and all kinds of government offices, like City Hall, where I work. We try not to waste anything."

I nod even though I already know this information.

"Maybe one day you'll work here in Silo, Yolanda," he says, smiling, then pointing down Commemoration Road, which connects to Remembrance. "We are expanding rapidly and will need bright young minds like yours to help in that growth."

"That would be nice," I say, relaxing a little.

"I've seen how committed you are in your Technologically Intuitive Education," he remarks. "You excel in your assessments, and you are always an eager participant in lectures. You have goals," he says. "I'm very impressed by your drive."

"You . . . you've seen my school scores?" I ask, surprised.

"I know all the top students in the System. That's how we recruit. Make sure you keep up those high marks, Yolanda."

My stomach sinks. He doesn't know I'm going to get kicked out if I can't pay for classes by tonight.

"Of course," I tell him as we approach the market.

"I'll walk with you to your stand," he says, starting off ahead. "Your sister is there, right?"

"Um, yes," I say, unsure how else to respond.

"Wonderful," he says, putting his hands behind his back as he walks. "It will be nice to say hello."

He looks ahead and smiles as he takes in Main Street. "We've come so far," he says wistfully. "I remember the tents. The frigid nights. The complete darkness and cold."

"You were there when everything went dark?"

"I was," he says, turning serious. "I was a little boy. Twelve or so. The storms across the country were relentless. Hurricanes on the coast. Freezes across the middle of the country. Twelve consecutive earthquakes that ripped a piece of the country off and sent it crumbling into the ocean. Everything lost connectivity. We had to survive without any power. Without knowing what happened to our neighbors, or our friends and families, far away, scattered and isolated across the continent. It was a brutal, brutal time brought on by Mother Nature's unforgiving force."

"Wow," I say, amazed and also kind of shocked Mayor Blackburn is sharing all this info with me.

We pass a building with a mossy exterior. It's the only fully green building in Silo. It looks like a forest of moss and vines enveloped the entire concrete structure. There is an archway in the middle that rises the length of the two-story building. Hanging vines dangle from the peak.

"Actually, it seems that I need to sign off on something first. I'll meet you at your stand afterward," he says, waving and smiling before disappearing inside the structure.

I walk past and see the sliding doors close behind him. The inscription on the glass reads:

THE EXCHANGE

My sister doesn't like that place. She says all the money in Silo runs through there. My sister hates money. She thinks it's pointless. But money will get me back into school.

Silo's market is lined up with stands all along Main Street. Self-driving vehicles, or SDVs, as most people call them, aren't allowed in town unless they're transporting materials for building. Most people walk. Some take hover carts and boards, but not even those are allowed on Main Street. Mayor Blackburn wants people to stroll on Main Street. He had a sign made that says:

STROLLING IN SILO IS SUPER

It's kind of, um, not the best sign. Maybe Mayor

Blackburn should stick to planning Silo's technological advancements and leave creating town signs to writers or something.

I walk along the middle of the street, looking at each stand. They're like one-story dollhouses for people living here to browse and play and buy things.

Up ahead, I see Mr. and Ms. Tanaka's stand. Ms. Tanaka and Abuelita were best friends. Mamá told me stories about how the two of them were among the first people to lay farm plots in the Valley—right around the time Silo was being built. Abuelita and Ms. Tanaka had been climate scientists studying hurricanes on an island south of the continent. That was before the tides rose and washed whole countries away.

When my parents were exiled, the Tanakas often came to check in on us and made sure we had enough to eat. I remember that first year, right before my seventh birthday, we had lost a whole harvest because of frost and they offered to take us into their home. Cami didn't want us to go and leave our family farm, but that didn't stop them from bringing us food, sugarcane water, and even sidings to cover holes that had sprung up around our house. But in all these years, they've never talked about my parents—just like Cami. It's like they never existed.

I approach their stand, and Ms. Tanaka immediately lights up.

"Yolanda! Tell me, have you gotten superiors on all your exams again?"

Ms. Tanaka gets right to the point with things.

"Yes, Ms. Tanaka," I tell her.

"Yolanda," she says firmly. "I have known you since you were *this* big." She practically touches the ground. "We're family. Call me Yui."

"Okay," I tell her for the hundredth time. I'm still not calling her by her first name though.

"So, what class will you be taking this term?"

I can feel my face tense up again.

"If we don't figure something out," I tell her, "I won't be able to afford to pay for my class. We don't have enough money to register."

"Maybe we can give you some. We have a little savings."

Mr. Tanaka pops up from behind a cart and waves.

"Hello, Mr. Tanaka," I tell him.

"How are you, Yolanda?"

Ms. Tanaka starts telling him about me not being able to register. He nods politely while his wife turns and takes my hand.

"We can give some money, Yolanda," Mr. Tanaka offers. "How much do you need?"

"Ten thousand credits."

It's five times the cost of any other class, but that's because it's the most advanced course that TIE offers.

Both of their expressions change. I know they don't have that much money.

"It's unbelievable," Mr. Tanaka says.

"How can the school charge that much?" Ms. Tanaka complains. "It's criminal!"

"Yui," Mr. Tanaka says, carefully looking around. "We don't want to bring unwanted attention."

Ms. Tanaka nods, eyeing one of the cameras on Main Street. She straightens up and puts her hand on my shoulder.

"We don't have that much, Yoly. I'm sorry."

"That's okay," I tell her, appreciating how they're always willing to help.

"Are you hungry?"

"A little," I tell them, and my stomach growls like it's getting impatient.

"We have some stalk if you want to take some."

Cane stalk isn't much better than Cami's protein bar, but at least it has a little sweetness.

"How much do I owe you?" I say, showing my V-probe to drop credits into their account.

Ms. Tanaka laughs a little, and Mr. Tanaka shakes his head and smiles.

"You know your money is not good here, Yolanda,"

Mr. Tanaka says, pointing to his stand.

I thank them and head back to our stand. Cami is still hopeful someone will want to buy at least one little fruit. She sees me approach, and I can tell by the look on her face that she hasn't sold anything. I grab a little white-and-pink strawberry and take a bite. Cami doesn't say anything. As soon as it hits my taste buds, I spit it out.

Sour. Very, very, very sour.

Unless someone has a craving for the tartest fruit ever, nobody is going to buy something they don't enjoy eating.

I look at my V-probe. Arelis isn't online. I can't tell if she got into our TIE class or not. Mayor Blackburn approaches our stand.

"Las hermanas Cicerón," he says cheerfully. "Hello, Camila." Mayor Blackburn looks at my sister's hand. "How's the augment holding up?"

Cami rubs her hand like it itches.

"It's fine, thank you."

"Good," Mayor Blackburn says. "Yolanda." He turns to me. "Did you know your sister was one of the first to have a successful augmented surgery here in Silo? After her unfortunate accident, we thought it would be good to use our rebuilding tech to help our fellow citizens who were injured in their service to their community."

Cami nods and rubs her hand like she's trying to rip

it off. I knew she got the augment after her return from Retreat. I didn't know she was one of the first successful augment surgeries. How could I know? It's not like she would have ever told me.

"How are you doing, Mayor Blackburn?" Cami smiles, but she's not comfortable. It's obvious with her blank stare and indifferent gaze.

"Fine, thank you. I had a lovely walk with your sister a short while ago," Mayor Blackburn says.

My sister's nostrils tighten, and she slightly clenches her jaw. It's subtle. The mayor doesn't notice. But I do. She's annoyed I didn't tell her about bumping into Mayor Blackburn. My sister doesn't like surprises.

"Market is almost done," he adds. "Are you all walking back to la finca?"

"Yes," Cami says.

"We could take an SDV to la finca, but Cami says it's too expensive," I add.

"Cállate, Yoly," Cami shushes.

I hate it when she tells me to shut up! Mayor Blackburn steps in before I can answer back.

"Your sister is right, Yolanda. It's not good to be wasteful. And this is one of the few times a year where walking is quite pleasant. Perhaps I can join you?"

"That's okay," Cami says, before Mayor Blackburn can

continue. "I'm sure you're very busy, Mr. Mayor."

"Well, yes," he says, "I am very busy, but not too busy to take a break and go on a nice walk. Here, I'll help you pack up."

Mayor Blackburn starts to collect the crates of strawberries and helps put them back into our hover cart.

"Not much luck at market today," he says, examining our crate. "Maybe there's something I can do to help."

"You've helped plenty, Mr. Mayor. Thank you."

Mayor Blackburn finishes helping us load our hover cart.

"Yolanda, I was thinking," he says seriously. "You can always ping me if you have questions about school."

"Thank you," I respond. "I really appreciate it."

"I know you do," he says, before turning to look at Cami. "I know you're under a lot of pressure, what with the farm and the strawberries and all that. But remember that I am here to help you both in any way I can. We have scholarships available for our very best students. I can certainly offer a recommendation."

"I'll find a way to pay for her classes, Mr. Mayor; thank you."

I can't believe Cami is telling him this. She was just saying we couldn't afford it!

"Cami, Mayor Blackburn is offering his help," I interrupt. "At least we should look into this scholarship."

I can see Cami tensing up again. I don't understand why she doesn't want to accept this opportunity for me to continue school! If I can become a neurolink surgeon, I can help by doing something I'm *good* at. I don't understand why she hates tech so much. It could be our way out of our dumpy old finca, where hardly anything grows.

Mayor Blackburn can sense the tension. He smiles and puts both hands together.

"I'll let you two discuss for a moment. I'm getting a ping about a query at the Exchange. Once you're ready to go, just send me a note and I'll come to walk back to the farm with you."

Mayor Blackburn leaves, and I can see Cami's nostrils are practically steaming from anger. My sister tries to hide her expression from everyone else in town, but I know her too well. She's upset but not as upset as I am. I don't understand why she has to hate everyone and everything so much. She doesn't trust *anyone*.

I get a buzz in my pocket and pull out my V-probe to see Mayor Blackburn has granted access to communicate.

The mayor's contact is still on my screen. Maybe he'll help. Maybe I can get a scholarship like he mentioned. I've never heard of a scholarship for school, but if Mayor Blackburn is offering it, it's because he believes in my potential. Not like my sister, who just says no to everything even though she doesn't have a plan herself. Cami is busy spraying the strawberries that are packed in the hover cart with water. As if that's going to make them more appealing.

People from Silo shop around, ignoring our stand completely. We're never going to sell enough strawberries to feel like we have a normal life. They just don't grow like they did when Mamá y Papá were around. Nothing has ever tasted the same. But maybe I can change our circumstances.

I swipe the contact and send Mayor Blackburn a ping. Taking the first step to making sure I get back into school and then to something better than a sad strawberry patch and a broken-down farm.

CHAPTER 3

The Choice

We end the day without having sold a single strawberry. Cami looks at her V-probe and then the sad crate. She offers it to the Méndez family.

"Gracias, Camila," Ms. Méndez says, accepting the crate.

We have plenty of crates, and she's really been struggling. Her two kids, Luciana and Marisol, are seven and eight, and she hasn't been able to earn enough credits to pay for their school. I can't imagine what I would have done if I couldn't have gone to school.

Luciana squishes her face once she tastes the strawberry. She hands a piece to her younger sister, who does the same.

They take turns sharing the strawberry until it's all gone. After they finish, they turn to their mother and ask for another. Ms. Méndez obliges, and the two siblings repeat sharing the strawberry back and forth between puckered lips and smiling faces. At least somebody's a fan of the tart flavor. I can't say the same thing for the rest of the people in Silo.

Ms. Méndez's orange groves haven't even produced naranja agria—the most bitter of all the citrus fruits. And their tomato plants are just shriveled-up vines snaking up and down trellises lining their property. I think their land might be worse than ours.

"Las niñas les gustan las fresas, Señora Méndez," Cami says, admiring the girls eating.

"They're sour," I say. "The strawberries. They don't taste great."

"That's okay, Yolanda. The kids like the pucker," Ms. Méndez says, offering another one to Marisol. She takes a bite, and her face squishes in, and her lips close tightly. Marisol chews and swallows the strawberry. Then she opens her hand and asks for more.

"Más, please." She puts another strawberry into her mouth and makes the same face again.

Ms. Méndez laughs. I don't get why she lets them eat the inedible fruit, but I guess it's nice to see them laughing and enjoying themselves.

"Gracias," Ms. Méndez says, taking Cami by the hand.

She squeezes warmly, and my sister offers a smile.

"You're welcome," Cami returns.

After we pack up our things, we say goodbye to a few neighbors as we wait for Mayor Blackburn to head out of town back toward la finca. I get a ping on my V-probe that shows his avatar, but I don't recognize the animal. It's like the head of a man with a cat's body. Maybe it's one of those genetic hybrid animals they created last century. I make a mental note to look up his animal avatar.

BURN1: Hello, Yolanda. So sorry, but a work thing came up. I'll meet you all back at la finca. I have good news for you and your sister!

He signs off my screen, which means I can't respond. I wonder what the good news is?

"Mayor Blackburn is running late. He says he'll meet us there."

Cami mutters something out of earshot, and again it seems like she's annoyed Mayor Blackburn is even coming to our house. I don't understand what her issue is with him. He's totally helpful!

"Vamos," Cami says, controlling the hover cart with her augmented hand.

"¡Vamos!" I say, excited to walk back home and wait for good news to arrive.

We approach the town gates, and the cameras above scan our V-probes. The penguin avatar appears again:

Produce sold—zero. Cash made—zero. Scholarship pending—ten thousand. Thank you for spending
your day in Silo, Camila Cicerón and Yolanda Cicerón.
We hope to see you again!

The second we step out of Silo and start down the road
toward la finca, Cami squeezes my hand.

"What did you do?" she whispers in an angry hush.

"It's nothing," I tell her. "Mayor Blackburn said he had
good news. That must be it!"

Cami keeps walking like she doesn't want to draw attention. She presses down on my hand like she used to when I
was little.

Cami looks behind, then to the side, like something is
going to pop out of nowhere and eat us.

"Why are you looking around like that?" I ask her, taking my hand away. "What is the matter with you, Camila?
You've been acting weird *all day*."

"Hablamos después," she says, whispering.

Cami walks ahead while I dig into my pants pocket
and pull out my V-probe. Arelis still isn't online. I scan
the school site but can't access the entry. The System is so
secure nobody can hack into it without getting caught. I
look at my screen and see the pending scholarship has just
been connected to my System account. Yes! It allows me
to see a teaser vid about the new classes I can take.

The familiar holograph of the redbrick building with

spires that reach the virtual sky comes into view. The programming team behind this is totally brilliant. I bet when I'm working in neurotech, I'm going to be friends with all these designers, programmers, and scientists. I'll be a neurolink surgeon living on Remembrance Road and buying whatever I want. Except a pheasant hat. That thing was awful.

Massive mahogany doors open once I scan across them. They lead to a cavernous hallway where professors step out of classrooms to greet me as I walk by. The class titles are prominently displayed above every classroom door:

QUANTUM COMPUTING

ADVANCED CODING LITERATURE

BRAIN COMPUTER INTERFACE

PRE-NEUROLINK STUDIES

ADVANCED NEUROLINK STUDIES

SYSTEM THEOLOGY

ANALYTICS

DEEP SEARCH DETECTION

RULES AND REPORTS

UPGRADES AND OVERRIDES

I've already taken Upgrades and Overrides and got the highest score of any student ever in Advanced Coding Literature, Brain Computer Interface, *and* Pre-Neurolink Studies. Arelis got the second highest. Not that we're competing. But Mayor Blackburn said the System notices top talent.

My panda avatar explores and wanders through the halls. Then I see it. The class I need to finally finish my TIE requirements.

Advanced Neurolink Symbiosis Analysis

15 hours

10,000 cr

Dr. Javier Sime—School of Advanced

Neurotechnology—Chair

Dr. Sime is the leading researcher in neurotech. He teaches the medical aspects of neurolink technology. I'll get to learn how to program the tiny device for AI to human symbiosis. I would even get to implant an actual link into a virtual human skull! That stuff was about to take off in the twenty-first century until, well, until everything went offline. But it's all coming back thanks to the System and brilliant scientists like Dr. Sime!

Maybe I'll be the one who develops some new AI interface that brings us back to the pre-midcentury era of advanced technology! Then Cami will finally see that my goals are worth pursuing. Dreams that can help us get out of this sad farm life we've been living in for so long.

I look back to my sister, who is quietly eyeing the road ahead. She stares at the sun dropping below the dirt road. The glimmer of light brightens her face. She has a few marks littered across her cheeks and under her eyes. But her scars have no voices—at least not ones that have ever spoken to me.

A chilly summer wind swoops in and kicks up some gravel at our feet. It tussles a few small rocks around, then swooshes back out to the Valley toward the mountains in the North. The temperature in the summer is always the same. Cool nights. Hot days. And winds that rush in and out from the neighboring mountains.

I hear people who live on the edge of the northern High Mountains don't get the same access to the System as people who live closer to Silo. Even with the WSE project trying to connect people out there. I feel kind of bad for them. How does their tech work without connection? How are they going to create or grow anything?

The Valley is a little over seven hundred square miles. There are hundreds of farms, each producing a different good. Mayor Blackburn says farmers are like artists. But really, we're just farmers.

When we get home, Cami sits on the porch steps and tells me to turn off my V-probe.

"Yoly." Cami grabs the V-probe out of my hands.

"Hey!"

I *hate* when she takes it from me. Like, despise it on a level I can't even explain.

"Give it back!"

She hands the V-probe over to me, and I secure it in my pants pocket.

"Don't scowl at me like that, Yoly," she says, staring. "I was trying to get your attention, and you weren't listening."

"Doesn't give you the right to snag my device."

"Fine," she says. "Just please turn it off."

"If I turn it off for more than five minutes—" I start, but she doesn't let me finish.

"I know. Just turn it off, and we'll bring you back online in two minutes."

"Fine."

Cami turns her V-probe off, and I do the same. She looks around like someone is listening nearby.

"I understand wanting to get into your neurotech class, Yoly. But you *cannot* accept an education scholarship, okay? It's dangerous."

"What do you mean it's dangerous? The Exchange gives me a scholarship; I use it to get an education. What's so complicated?"

Cami lets out a sigh, then hurries to speak.

"The Exchange doesn't *give* anything for free, Yoly. There's always a catch. Something you'll have to pay back."

"You're paranoid," I say. "And besides, even if there was a price, I'm going to get a job working in the System soon enough. I'm going to make a ton of credits and get us out of this dusty old farm."

Cami shakes her head.

"It doesn't work like that, Yoly—"

I don't let my sister finish. Instead, I push past her and run off toward the trees without another word. My sister doesn't want me to succeed. She wants to keep me stranded in this old finca forever.

I jump over the little fence that keeps our sad little strawberries. The tiny pollinator drones buzz around, avoiding me as I dart over the plants. Cami just wants everything to stay the same.

After a few minutes, I find the tree I used to climb with Papá and reach the first long branch. I move up the second, higher one, then the next. The higher I go, the more I hope the tree extends all the way back to Silo, where I can at least be around people who are like me. Not my sister, who will never, ever understand.

As night starts to fall, I can hear Cami calling out for me, but I don't respond. I tuck myself into the trunk of the tree, high above the ground. I've never gotten this far up before. I used to be too scared to climb this high.

I reach for my V-probe to check the details of my scholarship.

"Where is it?"

I dig around my front pockets and then my back ones. Then my heart starts racing. I left it on the porch when I ran off. It's been more than five minutes. Way more. The System issues infractions if we don't stay online. We can lose electricity from Silo's power grid if the infraction is severe enough. Mayor Blackburn says it's meant to protect us. To make sure we're all accounted for. To ensure nobody ever gets left behind again.

As soon as I start climbing down, I hear rustling in the fallen leaves. I stop on a branch and carefully try to see below. It's too dark to see from my height. The rustling continues, followed by a high-pitched giggle, then a deep low growl. I look down and see two glowing eyes staring at me in the fading sunlight. I recognize the features. A nightcat is pacing around the tree, its claws digging into the bark, looking for a way up.

I never thought a nightcat could be so close to our farm!

The cat leaps a few times, trying to get a grip on the tree. I move back. My heart is practically beating out of my chest. If it gets up the tree, there is no way I'll be able to get away. Maybe if I grab a branch and swing over to another tree.

It's hard to see. Night sets fast in the Valley. And the woods get dark before the rest of the countryside. The scratching continues below. A branch snaps, and the cat turns to see where the noise falls. It gets momentarily distracted.

I can see its spotted fur as it rummages around the bush where the branch fell. Now's my chance. I take a step and carefully feel my way toward the edge of the branch. The trees are tangled together; I can't exactly tell where one begins and the other ends.

"Easy, Yoly, easy," I say, trying to calm my nerves.

The branch seems sturdy. I grab a vine and tug a little. The nightcat paces. I hear it jump and claw at the bark again.

I leap across to the other tree. My foot lands on the branch. Then my other foot slips. I cling to the vine as both my feet lose balance. Instinctively, I wrap my wrist around the vine to secure myself from falling. My arm starts shaking. My wrist goes numb. I'm going to fall. There's no way I'll survive a fall like this. The nightcat is climbing the tree. I'm dangling, losing feeling in my arm.

"Yoly!"

Cami's voice carries through the dark.

"Cami! I'm stuck in a tree. There's a nightcat!"

Cami makes a high-pitched sound followed by a low growl. I hear the cat jump off the tree and land on the ground. The cat starts to make its creepy laugh again.

"Cami!"

Cami continues making her low-pitched growl. I can't see what she's doing, but I hear the cat repeating the sound

Cami is making. Then I hear a rustling in the bushes. The cat is growling and laughing.

"Cami!"

She doesn't answer.

I swing my body to the branch and finally get my footing again. My loose hand grabs another vine and I wrap my wrist around it, making sure I have my balance before unfastening my other hand. As soon as I do, I carefully make my way down to the ground.

"Cami!" I yell out, looking for her. "Cami!" I say over and over again.

I read nightcats work fast to devour their food. The thought makes my stomach turn.

"Cami," I whimper, seeing my sister lying on the ground. "No."

"No, what?" she says, standing up.

"It . . . it didn't attack you?"

"I know her," she says. "All she needed to do was smell me. She's more cat than hyena. Aren't you, sweetie?"

Cami strokes the cat's fur while I stand there completely shocked.

"Are you okay?" she asks, seeing me holding my wrist.

"Yeah, fine. Just a little sore from hanging fifty feet in the air."

"You could have gotten hurt."

"I know," I say, feeling bad for running away like that.

My sister takes my hand and examines my wrist. She squeezes it a little and then turns it around to check the pressure marks from wrapping my wrist around the vine so tightly.

"Pretty smart move wrapping the vine around your wrist like that," she says, impressed.

"Thanks, I guess?" I say, looking at my hand and rubbing my wrist.

Cami tells me the nightcat wasn't trying to eat me.

"She thought you were me," she says. "I've known her since she was a cub. Her mother was killed by hunters."

"Killed? How can someone kill an animal that big with their bare hands? Unless they trapped it or something."

"They shot it, Yoly."

Weapons haven't been around for as long as I've been alive. That was one of the more barbaric technologies of the last century. It's funny how so many incredible things were developed back then and also so many terrible things like weapons.

"But that's impossible."

"Weapons didn't disappear, Yoly. They just got retrofitted and stocked in places where most people can't get to them."

"Have you seen a weapon?" I ask, totally intrigued.

Cami doesn't answer. She looks away, then raises her hand out to the sky. She makes that same high-pitched laugh again, and something rustles in the bushes.

Bright eyes emerge from the shadows, and slowly, carefully, the nightcat comes to greet us. It's larger than both of us. I take a step back as it moves closer. Its round snout sniffs in my direction. It has teeth jutting from both sides of its closed mouth. It opens it and starts with its laugh-growl again.

"She's saying hi," Cami says, reaching out to pet the giant animal.

"Um, is that thing going to bite your hand off?"

"No, silly," she says.

The cat turns to me and moves toward my hand and sniffs.

"Keep your wrist facing down," Cami says. "Let her smell you."

"Cami," I say, moving slightly back. "You know how I feel about animals."

"Trust her," she assures me. "She's not going to hurt you."

I put out my hand as the cat continues sniffing my palm. I'm about to pull away again, but then the cat nuzzles into my palm and rubs its snout against me. It sniffs and licks my wrist. Then it moves in and leans its giant body against me. I hold its neck to stop me from falling. The cat doesn't back away.

"See?" Cami says as I rub the cat's coarse fur.

My heart continues to race as I pet this massive creature. Cami comes close and pets her also.

"We've known each other for a long time, ¿verdad, Chiquita?" Cami says, rubbing the cat's neck.

"Chiquita?"

"That's her name," Cami says.

"She's not very little," I tell her.

"She was when I found her," Cami explains. "She's been living in these woods for years. Since, um—"

"Since you left on Retreat," I say, completing her thought.

"Since I was *sent* on Retreat," she corrects, making sure I know she didn't have a choice.

CHAPTER 4

VOz

We leave Chiquita back in the woods and head back to la finca. The nightcat pounces into the shrubs and disappears into the trees.

"She eats little birds, mostly," Cami says. "She's adapting to climbing trees. There aren't many of her kind left. Their fur is sold in Silo."

"I've never seen fur sold on Main Street," I tell her.

Cami says the high-end markets have popped up around Remembrance Road. Beyond the mayor's mansion. I was just there and didn't see anything like that. I make a note to check it out when we go to Silo again. Then I remember my V-probe.

"My V-probe," I tell Cami. "I left it on the porch. It's

been off for two hours. I'm going to get an infraction!"

"You mean this one?"

Cami hands it back. There aren't any warning signs flashing across the screen. No search activations sent out to look for me. No infractions. Cami looks over my shoulder.

"The System might send an ambush drone if you're logged off for too long," she says.

"But that's to make sure we're safe. It's to keep us all connected."

Cami pauses like she's thinking what to say next. By the way she shifts around on our way back to la finca, I know she wants to tell me more. She glances at the V-probe.

"Sometimes the choices are made for you," she says, "but that doesn't mean you close your eyes."

I think about my sister's scars. About her augmented hand that she seems to despise. There's so much she hasn't wanted to tell me about her life before our parents were exiled. But maybe something's changing. I don't want to turn off the V-probe again, but I also want her to tell me more.

"Cami," I say, thinking about Chiquita, "maybe you can show me how to call her?"

She offers a smile and nods.

"Sounds like a plan."

We approach the strawberry field and step over the little fence. Cami leans over and runs one of the stems gently between her fingers.

"I doubt you remember our last really good harvest, years ago," she says. "Mamá y Papá took us to town, and we bought fresh sugarcane from the Tanakas, a handful of sweet oranges from the Méndez farm, and a bagful of almonds from Mr. McMillian's trees."

Cami picks a little strawberry and places it into her palm. I can't believe she's actually talking to me about the past! She's never shared *anything* about the time when we were all together as a family. I listen closely, hoping she'll tell me more.

"You were a baby, and Papá lifted you up to the sky," she continues, then smiles again. "And when you came down, he kissed your forehead. Then he threw you up in the air and hugged you all over again."

"And you made that high-pitched laugh like a night-cat!" I say, thinking I remember something like that. "Didn't I raise my hands up, wanting to be thrown in the air over and over again?"

Cami nods.

"It was bright and sunny," I recall. "I couldn't see your face well, but I knew you were smiling."

Cami smiles. She doesn't do it often, but when she does, it really lights up the sky.

A little pollinator drone zips around like it's out of control. It dives into the ground and gets stuck in the dirt. It buzzes and hums like it's trying to shake free.

Cami pulls the drone out of the dirt and inspects it using the light of the moon to see.

"Looks like they're glitching out again," she says, putting on a pair of bions to examine them.

"Let me see," I say, taking the little drone in my hand.

"Is it broken?"

"The microchip processor is on backward. The synthetic hair is supposed to be *on top* of the body, not on its *butt*."

Cami looks away, guilty.

"I tried," she says.

I shake my head while I unfasten the little plate with hair from the drone's bottom and refasten it on the top. "You know about animals and weapons and stuff, but not much about fixing drones."

"That's why I have you," she says, patting my back, admiring my work. "What's the prognosis, doctora?"

Cami watches me carefully. A smirk creeps onto her face.

"Did you fix it?" she goes on.

"Hand me your V-probe."

Cami places her device in my hand. I unlock it and open the icon that shows the pollinator operations, then reconfigure the drone's profile and update the software through the System's analytics drive. All the drones run through diagnostics. Sixteen green little dots on the screen light up, as their live tracking data runs underneath each of them.

I hand the V-probe back to Cami.

"You really are a whiz with this stuff, Yoly."

I shrug. "Basic programming stuff, no big deal."

I pretend like I don't appreciate the compliment, but I do. I really do.

The pollinator flies off and starts moving around the strawberry plants again. Even though the drones work, they don't do the job they need to. Which is pollinating strawberries that taste and look like actual strawberries.

"These drones no hacen nada."

"I know," she admits. "They are pretty useless."

The sound of humming echoes down the road from the farm. There's a cloud of dust kicking up as the humming continues. A black SDV turns onto our lot, hovers to our house, and stops near our strawberry fields. A door opens, and a pair of shiny boots steps out of the vehicle. Mayor Blackburn waves and smiles brightly.

"Las hermanas Cicerón," he calls out. "It's so nice to come out and visit la finca. I feel like it's been ages."

Mayor Blackburn approaches, and I notice the door. It stays open like the wing of a bird about to take flight. Mayor Blackburn notices me examining the SDV.

"We were able to decode the old programming software," he says. "From there, it was just giving them some tune-ups and a little love and care. We have a fleet of ten SDVs now. Isn't that incredible?"

"Yeah," I say, impressed.

"All salvaged from and around the Dead City. Three trucks. Five cars. And two cargo vans," Mayor Blackburn says, admiring the SDV. "The trucks took a little longer to fix, but we got them working. They're helping build Silo. One day soon, we'll be the shining example for a rebuilding world."

Mayor Blackburn approaches the front porch and says hello to my sister.

"You made it after all," Cami says dryly.

"I made a promise to visit. I like to keep my word. Tell me," he says, looking around, "would you like to reconsider my offer to upgrade the pollinators? We've uncovered some exciting new tech and think we're just months away from having far superior and efficient drones."

"We're fine, Mr. Mayor," Cami says shortly.

We're fine. She *just* admitted our pollinators are useless.

"Yolanda," Mayor Blackburn says, interrupting my thoughts. "I see you were offered a scholarship."

"Yes, thank you! I can't wait to log in and register for class."

"Excellent. I was happy to help."

"We haven't accepted the offer yet, Mr. Mayor," Cami interrupts. "We still have to look through the paperwork."

Mayor Blackburn holds the rail near the steps to the front porch. Cami is holding the same rail, looking directly at him. He takes a few steps and reaches Cami. He towers over her and never stops smiling. If I didn't know he was the mayor, he would look kind of scary standing over my sister like that. He looks out to me and nods.

"Yolanda has flourished under your care, Camila," Mayor Blackburn says. "I'm glad I was able to step in and help out. You were only seventeen, after all. Not quite an adult to oversee such a young child."

Cami looks uncomfortable. She turns away from the mayor and heads to the door.

"Yoly, let's get dinner ready. Mr. Mayor," she says in her most polite voice possible. "Thank you for coming by, but we can't accept the scholarship until we've had time to review it."

I walk up to the front porch.

"Yolanda," he says, angling his head down to make eye contact. "You are the type of mind we want in Silo. You remind me a great deal of myself when I was your age."

Cami is getting angry. It's always easy to notice by looking at how controlled her breath becomes when she's really upset.

"Thank you, Mayor Blackburn," I tell him.

"Of course," he says. "We look out for our community. Especially our future."

Mayor Blackburn heads back down the steps and toward the SDV. He looks around our fields, then out toward the edge of the woods near Abuelita's old shed.

"Your abuelita wrote a great deal about pollinators," he says. "Have you found anything in there that might help cultivate your fields?"

He points to the shed and then places his arms at his sides.

"Nothing," Cami says quickly. "Just dusty old furniture."

"And old papers," I offer. I hear Cami gritting her teeth so loudly it sounds like she's going to crush them.

"Old papers, huh? Have you read them?"

"Nah," I tell him. "It's boring stuff. Not like our TIE classes."

Mayor Blackburn's whole body shakes, and his deep laugh carries across our field.

"Ha! That's right, Yolanda," he says, hopping back into his SDV. "Make sure to accept the scholarship offer soon. If you wait too long, the Exchange will end up giving it to someone else, and I don't want you to miss out on the opportunity."

The door starts to drop closed.

"Take care, hermanas Cicerón. It was wonderful to see you."

The door closes, and the SDV hovers out of our driveway

and back to the main road to Silo.

"He's so nice," I say, watching the dust kick up from the SDV hovering away in the distance. The little pollinator drones start glitching out again. One of them just falls to the ground and powers down.

"Why don't you want to look into upgrades, Cami? You heard the mayor. There are new tech developments. We can totally start growing strawberries like we did back then!"

"I told you, Yoly, the Exchange doesn't give anything for free. We're not going to get any money from it. Stop asking about it," she says, walking out to the field and inspecting Abuelita's shed. "And you shouldn't be talking about Abuelita. Or her papers."

"Why not?"

"Because—" She catches herself before saying anything else.

"Figures," I mock. "Cami and her *razones*."

She exhales in her I'm-so-frustrated way, then walks back to the porch.

"Look at those patches over there." I point to the weeds overtaking some of the strawberry plants. "We could get some pesticide to kill them off."

"I'm not going to use neonicotinoids, Yoly."

My sister never took to using technology. The only cool tech thing she's got is that jacket of hers. And she's always wearing it. Like it's a survival thing or something.

"What if we buy agri-surveillance bots? Those are really good—"

She doesn't let me finish. She moves away and starts for the porch.

"Yoly, we are perfectly capable of *walking* out to the field, pulling the weeds with our bare hands, and adding nutrients to the ground to help the strawberries."

"If we upgrade the fleet, they might pollinate better. There are new models—"

"If we don't get a good harvest this season, we won't even be able to pay for the drones we have! Much less la finca to live in. Taking on more debt is not going to solve our money problems."

"What are you talking about? The System takes care of everyone."

Cami rubs her head and looks up to the sky like she wants to scream.

"We've run out of money, Yoly. We're two months behind on loan payments for those drones. And I have nothing left to pawn off."

Cami goes back up to the porch and taps on the doorframe to enter the house. It slides open, and she heads down the corridor leading to the kitchen. The information starts to sink in. If we lost our home, where would we live?

Another memory sneaks in. Mamá y Papá had been

gone for about a week. I was crying in my bedroom. Cami came in and tried to comfort me, but she didn't know how. She sat on the bed at first; then she leaned against me. I could feel her lower lip shaking a little. It was the only time I ever heard her cry. I had started to question if our parents *deserved* to be exiled. Whatever they did must have been really, really bad to receive such a sentence. But as easily as the doubt appeared, it went away. Our parents were good people. There must have been a mistake.

I asked Cami what had happened, but she couldn't answer me. She dried her tears and said, "It's you and me now, hermanita. We have to look out for the farm and each other."

It's funny how memories come back. Sometimes in pieces. Sometimes in complete pictures. I knew my parents weren't coming back. I knew my sister and I were all that was left of our broken little family. I just didn't understand why she cared so much about this farm. Why she *still* cares. The risk of losing it must be killing her.

I've focused on doing well in school. It's what I'm good at. But my sister has always put her attention to preserving la finca. How can you care about preserving a place that's a constant reminder of everything that went wrong?

I climb up the porch steps and swipe my hand to enter the house. Cami is quietly preparing food in the kitchen. All we eat are modified beans and vitamin supplements with water. That's something we have plenty of—water. Cami says we're lucky because without water, we couldn't survive. I'm starting to feel like money is more important to survival than water.

Cami doesn't look up when I walk in. I decide to go to my room and see if Arelis is online. So much has happened since this morning, I almost feel like it's been forever since we spoke.

I go to my room and wave the lights on.

"Video," I command the wall screen.

The wall lights up and sends a buzz to my V-probe. The V-probe routes everything to the System. The wall responds by blinking a few times, then opens the conferencing application.

"Who would you like to video conference?"

"The same person I call every single day of my life, VOz," I tell the wall screen.

"Please specify username."

"Ugh, video conference ARE122107," I say, throwing myself on my bed. "The software on these probes needs to be more intuitive."

"Conferencing," VOz says in that gruff voice she's programmed to speak in.

I look around to see if Arelis's going to pop up, but the line keeps moving across the screen. It's hard to get a call to connect where she lives, which is why we usually just chat. But I feel like seeing a friend.

I really wish she would answer! It rings, and I get a pause before the connection comes on. Arelis's face pops up on the screen. The video is grainy. It isn't coming in good quality.

"¡Amiga!"

"Hey, Yoly."

She looks strange. Like she got ran over by an SDV tractor or something.

"Hey, ¿qué pasa? You don't look so great."

"I'm fine," she says, rubbing her eyes. "Been working on this new thing. It's almost ready."

Arelis is a genius at gadgets. She once retrofitted a pair of boots to be self-tying. Like midcentury gadget–level cool. Technically we're not supposed to do unauthorized programming, but she got away with it because she said it was a project for school.

I notice her face looks tired. Like she wants to keep talking but doesn't have the energy.

"Hey? Are you okay?" I ask.

"Yeah," she says softly. "This device is going to, um—"

Arelis leans into the camera. Her eyes get a little wider. More awake. She looks around, then nods her head like she wants to tell me something, but instead she stays quiet like she's holding a secret she wants to let out but can't. She seems stressed and worried, so I decide to change the subject.

"You wanna watch *The Scourge* again?" I say, trying to cheer her up. Honestly, there is so much to talk about, but I don't want to weigh her down with my stuff when she looks like she's got a lot on her mind right now. Besides, a little binge read about killer insects of the last century with my best friend is exactly what I need right now.

"Sounds good," she says, looking like she's forcing herself to cheer up.

I turn the camera to face the wall. Arelis doesn't have a wall screen at her house. She told me that it would be pointless to get one because connectivity is so bad in the Outer Valley.

"I hear the WSE might be working on connecting fiber-optic cables down by you," I tell her while adjusting the camera so she can see better. "Maybe they'll be able to repurpose those old silos that never went online too? Then you'll have a total System connection upgrade!"

"Nobody here wants the WSE or the loans they're coming with, amiga."

"How do you mean?"

"Cornelius and a whole bunch of folks in the neighborhood are refusing loans to run additional optic lines over here. WSE folks aren't too happy. I don't know. Maybe soon we'll be able to connect easier."

The screen gets grainy, and I can barely see her face.

"Arelis? Hey, can you hear me? Hello?"

The screen goes dark for a moment, then lights up again.

"Hello?" I say, checking the connectivity. I have full power. There shouldn't be a lag. My V-probe starts buzzing, then my wall screen flickers. "Arelis? Can you hear me?"

"Amiga," I hear her say, moving close to the video. "The icon," she says, then starts to cut out. The screen blurs; then she briefly comes back into view. "Make sure you log—"

The screen goes blank. She's disconnected.

"VOz, video conference ARE122107."

VOz comes back online.

"*The Scourge*," she says from the speakers in the corners of my room. "Written by Hortensia Blackburn. Chapter One—"

"No, I don't want *The Scourge*," I order VOz. "Stop. Stop narration! Video conference ARE122107."

"Where would you like to skip to?"

"Stop the reading. VOz, STOP."

I look around the walls. The cover of *The Scourge* floats on the wall near the far side of the room. "Chapter Twenty," VOz continues. "Evil Insects of the Past."

"STOP. Command STOP!"

VOz continues to narrate and display images from the book.

Insects fly around. The speakers hum with different

sounds. From the corner of my room, a buzz rings in my ear. I jump back.

"Whoa!"

A massive insect swarms around the walls of my room. There are spiders spinning giant webs inside homes, mosquitoes drawing blood on human skin, and a giant green-looking thing called a mantis that appears to be eating its own kind!

"VOz, COMMAND STOP," I continue. Why isn't she responding? I look at my V-probe and see the application can't be logged off. It isn't letting me message Arelis either. She said to log in, but to where? She could have been talking about school. It's the only other application we're normally on together. I click on the TIE app and scroll to see there's only one spot left in the class.

That must be what she was trying to tell me! She must have been warning me that the class was almost full. I try to call her back, but the connection is lost. Ugh!

I move my avatar closer to the class. But I'm locked out. I can't access the room. VOz continues narrating *The Scourge* in the background.

"And the worst of all abominations," VOz carries on, "was the killer of plants, the tormentor of crops. . . ."

"The bees!" another high-pitched voice yells from the narration.

"Jeez, that's annoyingly melodramatic," I say, trying to

figure out how to disable the wall screen. A bee continues buzzing around menacingly. It lands on flowers and chews down on the petals, leaving mucus all over the plant.

I look up from my V-probe to the wall as VOz continues to narrate. The bee is now using its giant stinger to inject a human hand. The guy's hand swells up like a balloon. He runs around screaming in pain.

"The sting of the evil bee will cause the skin to . . ."

There's a pause in the narration. The image pans to the guy's face. His look of terror says it all. His hand is going to—

"Explode!" the screeching voice blurts out.

I never realized how obnoxious of a writer Hortensia Blackburn is. Arelis and I used to crack up at the loud shrieks; now they are just annoying. I reach under my bed and find the processor that runs VOz and detach the main box. My V-probe lights up, and I examine the mainframe. The microchips are humming along together. It's like VOz is breathing.

I swipe a few codes and point my V-probe at the box but can't get access to the internal processor. The image projects the list of codes. I pull a cable to disconnect VOz, but it's locked into the electric outlet under my bed. Dust mites tickle my nose, and my neck starts to itch.

I get a ping on my V-probe.

"Arelis!" I say, looking. But it isn't Arelis. It's a message from the Exchange. It flashes across my screen:

Your scholarship for 10,000 is waiting to be claimed! To begin money transfer into your System account, please have a guardian click AGREE on the button below. Offer must be accepted within twenty-four hours. Congratulations!

CHAPTER 5
The Promise

I pace around my room trying to figure out what to do. I don't want to miss out on getting into this class. This is my only shot. To finish school and be on my way to securing an apprenticeship before finally becoming a neurolink surgeon!

I look back at the screen. It says I need a guardian to agree, but Cami won't ever say yes. I could try to press AGREE—no one would know that it wasn't Cami who hit the button—and if there is a guardian-verification security, I could try to crack it. Then the scholarship funds would be transferred immediately.

But my sister's nagging voice in my head tells me I should read some of the details. There's a tiny icon that reads TERMS. It opens when I click on it, and I read through the first two paragraphs. It doesn't really say anything out of the ordinary. Stuff like "duration of the scholarship," "extensions," and "processing of funds."

"There's nothing here that's dangerous," I say out loud.

"What was that?" Cami calls out from the kitchen.

I look back at the screen and press AGREE.

The screen pings and my account says: 10,000-TIE Scholarship Fund.

"It let me agree," I say, happy but surprised there wasn't even a password-protected guardian code or something.

I need to figure out how I'm going to keep this from Cami. It's not like I can tell her the truth; she'd only get upset.

As if reading my mind, my sister knocks on the door and asks to come in. The door slides open before I can answer.

"Hey," I say, removing my headset. I lie on my bed and pretend to start up VOz again.

"Did you talk to Arelis?"

"Yeah," I tell her. "But we got cut off. Connection stinks."

Cami moves into my room and takes a seat on the edge of my bed.

"Hmm," she says. "I'll try Cornelius later. They've been getting outages over there. It's hard to find out exactly what's going on."

She talks with Cornelius all the time. They're tight like me and Arelis. It's how we ended up in school together. They enrolled us in the same classes. Cami looks at my V-probe. I flip it over so she doesn't see the available credits on my screen.

"I have to go into town tomorrow. I need to check something at the Exchange."

"I'll come with you," I say, thinking I can shop for materials for class. I bet Arelis already has everything. She has a way of getting stuff even though she's so far away from Silo. I think about how quickly she cut off. It was probably just a random lost connection. I'm sure she'll turn up in class tomorrow morning.

"Yoly, I'm sorry I didn't tell you that we were running low on money and weren't going to be able to re-enroll you in school. I knew how much you wanted to get into that neurolink class. I didn't want to disappoint you."

"It's fine," I say, lying. I've never lied to my sister. My pulse quickens. It's a combination of excitement and guilt.

Cami pats my foot.

"I started thinking about something Abuelita used to say."

She hasn't spoken about our grandmother in a really long time. Cami said she left a few years before I was born. I know she died, but Cami never likes saying that word. She just tells me she's "gone." That's why I'm sure she doesn't believe our parents have survived being exiled either. I try not to think about it. Better to push it away.

"Abuelita used to say," Cami continues, "lo que tienes es lo que necesitas, y lo que necesitas lo buscas."

That's what I've done, I think. I needed to get into school, so I found a way to do it. Cami continues telling me about Abuelita.

"She always told me what we need is right in front of our eyes. We just have to search it out. For years I've wondered what that was, what she meant. I think I finally figured it out after years of searching."

"What is it?"

Cami looks around and then quietly pats my ankle.

"I'll tell you later," she says, looking around like she's trying to avoid something. She turns back to me and gives me one of her concerned looks. "Yoly?"

"Yeah?"

"Promise me you won't take that scholarship from the Exchange until we've read through every detail in the contract?"

"I promise," I say, lying for the second time. My sister doesn't notice. It doesn't feel great, but I know my plan will help us in the long run. Better to just make it happen and then tell her later. She'll understand eventually. Cami leaves my room while I check my V-probe. I log in to school and find Dr. Sime's neurolink course. I click on the pay tab:

ADVANCED NEUROLINK SYMBIOSIS ANALYSIS—

credits—10,000

    Scholarship balance: 0

    Remaining money: 0

CHAPTER 6

Cause and Effect

The next morning, I get up early and log in to class. Dr. Sime's class is designed like a lab. There are three-dimensional skulls in front of each desk, along with a tiny chip that's meant to be inserted into the skull and activates the neurolink.

Dr. Sime doesn't waste any time to start teaching. He gives a brief lecture about the neurolink being an invention of the early twenty-first century. Then he goes on about the tech being forgotten when the environment collapsed but how now it's being rebuilt through the System for the betterment of humanity.

"The neurolink," he says, "connects us all through our brains. It provides health benefits beyond the measure of the natural world. It is the next step in our evolution. Finally, thanks to the great technological archaeologists here in Silo, we've been able to begin the redevelopment of the neurolink technology. Some of you will one day receive the medical certification to perform the neurolink surgery implants. Only a select few of you will be awarded that distinction."

I was kind of hoping I'd see Arelis in class, but she wasn't there. Even when connection has been bad, Arelis has always managed to reach out. But she still hasn't responded to any of my pings. I get a sinking feeling in my stomach.

According to Cami, the Outer Valley has been experiencing more blackouts lately. So it's likely that Arelis is trying to figure out the problem right now. I'm sure she's fine. Still though, I wish her pings were coming through.

There are only a few students in the class. They're sporting expensive skins. This one kid named EmpRess has a white hood with feathers running down the back. I can't see their face, and they didn't answer when I said hello. It's strange that they aren't using a standard username.

Dr. Sime's avatar has a lion's body and a human head. He doesn't move at all and, besides lecturing about the first bit of neurolink information, he barely speaks. When he does talk, it's usually in one or two sentences like, "Make an incision in the cerebral cortex and implant the device." That's it.

By the time class is over, I'm completely lost. I ended up making an incision too high up, and my test skull started shaking. A big sign flashed across my screen saying:

Your patient is deceased. Neurolink operation—
failure.

Dr. Sime doesn't stop to help me. The other students are private chatting and don't bother to even ask my name. They're kind of snobby, but I'm not about to let their attitude get to me. I'm here to pass the class and stay on the path that will eventually lead me to a job at the neurolink medical center in Silo. I don't need to make friends. I just need to work hard.

I step out of the class and log off the school site. The System returns to my home screen. The scholarship balance is permanently displayed on my upper screen. Like it's reminding me I already spent everything. If Cami sees it, she's going to freak out. I have to make sure to hide my V-probe screen from her. I look out the only window in our house and see the sad little drones doing their best to pollinate our strawberries.

Cami greets me when I walk into the kitchen area. She's just finished brewing some herbal tea, and honestly, it doesn't smell very good.

"What is that?"

"Good morning to you too," she says sarcastically. "You were up early," she adds. "What were you doing?"

I inspect the drink in her hand.

"What is that floating in there?" I say, changing the subject.

"It's calendula tea," she says, showing me. "A little bitter but a good anti-inflammatory. And apparently good for diaper rashes." Cami laughs. "Abuela taught me. She said I used to get pretty severe diaper rashes when I was little."

She hands me a piece of paper. Like, actual real paper they used over a hundred years ago!

"Where did you get this?" I say, feeling the smooth texture.

Cami puts one finger to her lips to hush me. She points to the paper and tells me to read it. It's written in ink, which is difficult to decipher. I recognize a word:

Abuelita

Cami and I make eye contact. She points to the paper again.

"I don't understand," I tell her, frustrated and annoyed she isn't telling me where she got the paper. I ask her again, but she just points to the letter.

She realizes I can't read it, so she goes outside and tells me to follow her. We go down the porch step and out to Abuelita's shed. She looks at my V-probe, and I quickly move it away. Cami gestures for me to turn it off. I do what she says and power it down. We have a few minutes.

"Okay, it's off. Now can you tell me?"

"So last night," she starts excitedly, moving her hands for emphasis. "After, um, Mayor Blackburn left." She makes a face like she's tasting something gross. Maybe it's her tea, I joke to myself. "I was thinking about Abuelita," she continues. "I remembered she used to make tea every morning. She even made chickweed tea once!"

"What's that?"

"It's in tall grass. Sticks to you if you walk through it. Great drink for energy in the morning."

I look at my V-probe. I can't be offline for much longer.

"And the paper?"

"It's in Abuelita's old shed. Anyway, I went in there last night. There's something I want to show you. There are a lot of scientific words and jargon that you might be able to help out with."

"Like what?" I asked, intrigued.

"Abuelita wrote about these woods, Yoly. About—" She looks around again like she thinks something is eavesdropping. "Something that might help us get out of debt."

"The woods?" I say, pulling back. "With that giant nightcat out there? No, gracias."

"Chiquita isn't dangerous, Yoly. You know that."

"What about hawks? Or deer."

"Hawks are hardly big enough to hunt you, and deer are not dangerous."

"What about other nightcats? They're not all friendly."

"I've never seen another nightcat in our woods. And believe me, I've explored these woods."

What she says makes me think of the times Papá and I used to play by the edge of the trees. Climbing and collecting dirt. Mud didn't bother me so much when I was little. Now I hate it. It gets in my fingernails and is impossible to wash off. Plus, there are roaches and other nasty insects in the dirt.

"There's an old wooden box in the shed," Cami continues. "There are slats inside it and a little opening on the side. And," she says, looking around again, "there's a journal and a book."

"A book? Like a real book?"

She nods.

"About what?"

"They're both about bees," she says, pulling the journal out from her jacket.

She opens it and shows me a drawing of a box with a picture of one of those death insects on the corner of the page.

"Cami," I say, ignoring the journal and looking at my V-probe. I have to turn it back on before the System flags me. "Why would Abuelita write about some extinct killer insects? And why do you think it, or whatever's *supposedly* in the woods, is going to be of any use to our money problems?"

"I don't know," she says, looking out to the woods. She seems lost in thought while I stand near the porch next to Abuelita's shed noticing the splinters jutting out of the floorboards. The patchwork of a house we live in is made up of cinder blocks on one side and logs of wood on the other. Our roof has two large slats of aluminum sealed together with concrete and a solar panel that hasn't been updated since I was a kid. We have one window that looks out to the sad strawberry fields and a kitchen that is connected to a living space with a small hall that separates our bedrooms.

The homes in Silo seem so much more developed than our early century farmhouse. They have large glass windows and brick that was transported from the Dead City. The Valley farms are all old and decaying. At least Silo is using materials that haven't gone completely to waste. If my plan works out, I bet we can live in one of those new two-story apartment lofts near Remembrance Road. I look back at my sister, still staring out into the woods.

"Even if reading some science book Abuelita wrote did lead us somewhere, we don't know whether it'll be to anything worth trading for in Silo. It isn't going to fix the very real money problems you talked about yesterday, Cami."

My sister seems dejected. Her good mood gone. She returns to the scowl I'm used to seeing.

"This is why no te digo nada."

"I don't need you to tell me anything, Cami," I say to her, getting upset. "You spend six years not telling me things, and one magical evening with a killer animal and the mayor mentioning Abuelita, and suddenly you're showing me some *journal* she wrote a *long time ago* and asking me to *decipher* all these scientific and technical terms you don't understand because there could be *some clue* in there that *might* help us. Sorry, pero no gracias. *I* actually did something to help our circumstances."

Cami's eyes train on mine. She hardly even blinks.

"Did you . . . ," she says, stepping close. "Did you accept that scholarship? Tell me you didn't, Yoly."

I shield my V-probe from her.

"No! Just leave me alone."

"Yolanda," she says, serious. "Let me see your V-probe."

"No!"

I move away from her, but she quickly steps closer to me. Her hand gets hold of my wrist. Her metal augmented fingertips tighten around it.

"Let go of me!"

I push her off. She stumbles back. My wrist feels sore. I look at her metallic hand.

"I'm sorry," she says. "I didn't mean to hurt you."

"You're not Mamá. You don't get to decide what I do with my life!"

"Yoly," she says, trying to soften her tone. "Please trust

me when I tell you, accepting things like scholarships from the Exchange is not good. Tell me you read the fine print. The rules for accepting the money. Please tell me you read them before you agreed?"

Cami doesn't understand that my plan is better. I can get us out of this farm. Move us to Silo. Give us a better life. She would rather stay in this shabby old house forever.

"I'm not like you, Cami. I'm good at school. I can make something more of myself. The System will give me a job. We'll have enough money to live on Remembrance Road and—"

Cami steps closer.

"Can I please read the terms of the scholarship?"

Cami reaches out. My sister has always been distant. She told me to go to school, help out on the farm, do my chores, go to sleep. All she's done is boss me around. Never talking to me about anything. Now she just wants me to trust her when all she's done is put us into more and more debt? No way.

"Get away from me!" I tell her, running off.

"Yoly!" she says. I hear the footsteps behind me. My sister is fast. Way faster than I am. Within seconds, I feel her metal hand on my shoulder. She doesn't press down, but I feel the weight anyway. I push her off and turn to face her.

"No matter how well I do in school, you always go back to me working around la finca. You never support *my* dreams. Why don't you? ¿Por qué no crees en mí? ¿Por qué?"

Her face softens, and my grip on the V-probe loosens. She already knows I agreed to the scholarship. There's no point in hiding it anymore. I show her the screen. She takes the V-probe in her hand and stares at it for a long time. She clicks on a few buttons and starts scrolling.

"What are you reading?" I ask, leaning in to see.

"The agreement you accepted," she says. Her voice sounds firm. Like she's analyzing something without much emotion. Once she's done scanning the agreement, she hands the V-probe back.

Her face changes. It's a face I know all too well. "Yoly, by accepting—" she continues before stopping to watch me carefully. It's the pause she always gives when she wants to make sure I understand what she is telling me. Her face is tight, and her mouth hardly moves before she continues. "Yoly, you have to do time on Retreat as repayment."

"What?" My neck tightens, making it difficult to catch my breath. "But I'm on the track to become a neurolink surgeon. Mayor Blackburn said I'm a promising youth."

"Mayor Blackburn needs youth out beyond the Valley, Yoly. That's what I was trying to tell you." She starts picking at her nails and then rubbing her scalp. "Yoly, after you're done with the class, you have to serve time. They're going to send you beyond the Valley—to the Dead City.

You're going to do time on Retreat."

The words land like a windstorm tearing through me. I didn't read the full contract. My palms are full of sweat. My heartbeat quickens. She's never explained why she was sent on Retreat. But I know it wasn't a good experience. She has scars from her time there. And not just small ones.

A big burn scar runs from her rib cage down her leg. The scar is jagged. Like a twisting road. I must have been eight when I asked her what happened, but she dismissed my question. All she said was, "Don't ever touch a loose wire."

"Cami," I tell her, feeling like I'm about to faint. "The class finishes in six months."

Cami tries to calm me down but isn't having much luck. I can't believe I didn't read the full agreement.

"Mayor Blackburn will help. He knows I'm a good student. Maybe he'll make an exception."

"He already made an exception. They don't care how good someone's grades are, especially someone outside of Silo. They just care about having enough kids to send out to scavenge," Cami says, then goes back to planning. "Maybe since I'm your legal guardian I can say you agreed without my approval. Try to cancel the class."

I open my V-probe and log in to class. I try to unenroll myself, but it doesn't let me withdraw.

Request DENIED

I read the class description, scanning for information

about canceling or maybe withdrawing. There's nothing. I read a little more and see some writing in a much smaller font. It's hard to see what it says. I zoom in and read the small print.

Class cancellations not permitted.

"It won't let me cancel the class. Cami, what am I going to do?"

"If we act quickly, there might be time to refund the transaction. I know someone in the loan department at the Exchange. Her name is Lucía. Maybe she'll help. There might still be time to reverse this."

I nod, feeling terrible as we jog down the road and toward the main strip that leads to Silo.

The Sánchez family finca comes up in the distance. They have rows and rows of corn, but most of the stalks don't really yield edible corn. We had one bad wind season a few years ago—five consecutive tornadoes swept through the Valley. It was scary. Luckily the woods provide a natural protection from windstorms and tornadoes. Unfortunately, the Sánchez family finca is right on the road to Silo. The tornadoes destroyed their crops. They've never fully recovered.

There's an old-looking autotractor puttering along the fields, messing up cornstalks instead of pulling weeds like it's supposed to. An SDV zips by carrying passengers. I don't recognize the faces of the people inside; for a moment it looks like one of the passengers has a metallic face. Impossible. Nobody has been able to figure out the midcentury programming for cyborg enhancements.

We approach a little marker in the road.

LOT 2506—FAMILIA CICERÓN

The massive conifers making up our forest block out most of the sunlight under their canopy of branches and leaves. It covers the length of our farm, save for the little plot dedicated to the strawberry fields. My V-probe is flashing again. The loan amount pops up on my screen. I don't want to admit it, but I should have known better. I should have read the fine print!

"Hey," Cami says, interrupting my worried thoughts. "If refunding the scholarship doesn't work, we have something else we can explore." Cami looks out to the woods, then puts her finger to her lips to make sure I don't say anything out loud.

My sister's augmented digits move away from her mouth as she continues quietly down the road. I can't believe that Cami, who up until yesterday had rarely spoken even a single word about our grandmother, is still going on about Abuelita leaving some clue for us years ago.

How is something that has to do with bees of all things supposed to be our *plan B*?

CHAPTER 7

Shadows and Memories

I see Silo's Welcome Center on my V-probe as we approach the town gates. The little penguin signals our arrival:

> Welcome, Camila Cicerón and Yolanda Cicerón of Lot 2506. Please state your business in Silo in the System portal.

Cami swipes into her V-probe, then puts it back inside her jacket. We walk into Silo and head toward the Exchange.

"Let's see what Lucía says," Cami reassures. "We met on Retreat. She helped treat my injury."

I look at Cami's arm again, where her metal meets her skin. I can't imagine what it must have felt like. My sister has told me more in these last few days than ever before. I wonder what got her to start opening up? As if reading my thoughts, she answers.

"I *know* I should have told you more," she says as we approach the Exchange. "Okay?"

"Okay," I say, appreciating even a little admission of her secrets.

We reach the mossy entrance to the Exchange.

"Stay here," she says. "I'll go speak to Lucía."

I decide to walk down to Main Street while I wait. There are a few people gathered around a platform hovering above the street. Mayor Blackburn is waving to everyone. People wave back and clap as he salutes the crowd. They're people who live in Silo. I can tell by their flashy clothes.

"Good people of Silo!" he bellows into the microphone attached to his ear and chin. The sound carries across Main Street and through the alleyways in town. It's so loud I jump back. There's a tiny speaker in the shrubs, and I can see there are at least five other sound systems nearby. My V-probe flashes, and I see the mayor's speech broadcasting on the System. I've never heard him speak in real life before. I've always just seen him when the System plays his weekly "connectivity checkups" to the Valley. I look back to the floating platform as Mayor Blackburn looks to one of the screens capturing the video that's broadcasting through the System.

"Many of you out in the Valley have fallen onto hard

times. Agribusiness is down; you're behind on loans, running into massive amounts of debt that is impossible to be repaid."

He keeps talking to the camera that's broadcasting to everyone in the Valley.

"Our first goal as a community," he continues, "is to take care of each other. Especially when times are tough. With that in mind, I'm implementing a flat pay for everyone living outside of Silo. This will begin next week."

Mayor Blackburn continues talking about the flat pay. He says that every homestead living in the Greater Valley will receive fifty thousand credits to cover costs, no matter what crops they're producing or not producing. I see someone from the Valley watching the mayor talk. It's strange for both of us to be here when it's not market day. Usually, people from the Valley come to town only on the weekends. He sees me and I wave.

I think his name is Andrés. He's a little older than me—maybe fourteen. I walk over just as two scary-looking drones hover toward him. The crowd moves back while the drones release four extensions from the sides of their bodies and corner Andrés into a wall.

"Business not stated," one drone reports.

"System override detection," the other one says.

The mayor notices and stops talking. The cameras turn off, and the System feed stops the broadcast. He steps off the platform and makes his way through the crowd. Nobody says anything. Andrés stays quiet.

"What's going on?" Mayor Blackburn says, approaching Andrés. "Stand down," he orders the drones.

The drones obey his command and drop their extensions to their sides. I've never seen drones like this before. They hover aboveground and have sleek, white cylinder-like bodies with heads that look like domed helmets. There are screens for their faces that squiggle when they speak. I remember all kinds of drones were mass-produced last century. But they mostly ended up as scrap over the years. These things look different. Like they were patched together and reprogrammed into something more menacing.

"These are our brand-new Artificial Intelligence Force drones," Mayor Blackburn says, addressing the crowd. "AIF for short. We've just finished development and are ready to deploy them for the safety and well-being of our community."

Mayor Blackburn turns back to Andrés. He commands the AIF out of the way.

"Young man," he starts. "Market days are on weekends. What brings you to Silo on an off day?"

Andrés doesn't answer. He moves his hands like he's trying to communicate, but the mayor doesn't seem to understand him.

"Young man," Mayor Blackburn continues. "Please answer the question." .

Andrés continues to move his hands like they're his voice. Like he's saying whole sentences with his gestures.

"Why are you signing, young man," Mayor Blackburn asks, sounding slightly annoyed, "when you have a perfectly capable device to communicate?"

He points to Andrés's V-probe and motions for him to use it.

"Just turn the volume up and we'll hear you just fine."

I can see Andrés looking at Mayor Blackburn's lips. It's like he's trying to figure out what he's saying. The mayor points to the V-probe again.

"Use that," he says, emphasizing with his fingers to his palm.

Andrés looks at his V-probe, then at the drones, and then back at the mayor. He shakes his head, then continues to look around nervously.

"Young man, we cannot have unauthorized visitations into town. Everyone is required to register with the Town Welcome Center. Do not avert your eyes. I'm speaking to you."

Andrés is not looking at Mayor Blackburn. He's shifting his eyes downward and is starting to shake his head. I want to do something, but I don't know how to help him. Just as the mayor is about to speak again, I hear someone calling from across Main Street.

"Andrés! Andrés!"

It's Ms. Martínez. She runs across the street and pushes through the crowd to get to her son. She reaches him and hugs him. He doesn't hug her back, but I see he puts his head on her shoulder. She moves her hands like he did, and he responds with his own gestures.

Ms. Martínez turns around and faces the mayor.

"I'm sorry, Mayor Blackburn. He . . . he wandered off. Disculpe."

The mayor moves in and pats Andrés's head. Andrés doesn't respond.

"That's okay, Señora," he says. "I was just worried about the boy. I don't want him to get hurt."

"Thank you, Mr. Mayor," she says, then signs something to Andrés. He responds angrily, then shakes his head and storms off.

Ms. Martínez follows her son. She's careful not to bump into the drones. She catches up to Andrés and starts for the exit but is stopped by Mayor Blackburn.

"Seems he has some trouble with the V-probe speech application," he says. "We'll be sure to have our programmers develop something that can be useful for his communication needs."

He doesn't have a problem with communicating, I think. You just don't understand his language.

"We're going to help take care of you and your boy, Ms. Martínez," Mayor Blackburn calls out. "I know the challenges you face. We just want you to know we're here for you."

"Gracias, Señor. Take care."

Ms. Martínez starts off again. She glances up and sees me watching. Her look changes a little. Like she's switched from worried into something even more serious. She nods in my direction, and I offer a small wave. Andrés sees me and seems to recognize something. He offers a wave and for the first time, I notice a scar that seems to run the length of his arm all the way to his neck.

I smile back at him. Ms. Martínez leaves, passing under the Welcome Sign, and disappears down the road. Mayor Blackburn approaches behind me.

"Miss Cicerón," he greets me. "I see you're in town to visit the Exchange."

"Yes, sir," I tell him, not sure if I'm allowed to be here or not. "My sister is . . . she's checking on something."

"About your school? She's asking the clerk Lucía about your scholarship, correct?"

I nod, surprised he knows exactly why we're here.

"Lucía is from the Outer Valley. Did you know that?"

"Um, I didn't," I tell him.

Mayor Blackburn takes a bite out of something I don't recognize.

"Even folks from all the way out there can make a nice life here in Silo!"

He takes another bite, and I can smell a sweet aroma coming from the inside.

"A pear," he says, showing me. "Can you believe we've managed to produce a pear in our Silo greenhouse?"

"Is it a fruit of some kind?"

"Exactly, Miss Cicerón," he says, taking another bite. "You're very smart."

Mayor Blackburn keeps eating the pear and marveling at how good it is. He says the new pollinator drones the tech labs have built have worked to pollinate dozens of fruit species that haven't been around for decades.

"After years and years of retrofitting and building and modifying the past models," he says, admiring the pear again, "we finally have drones that can do the job. We're going to be flight-testing them in about a month. Isn't that wonderful?"

I nod, unsure what he means about flight-testing a whole bunch of pollinator drones.

"So, about school," he says, turning more serious. "I know it must seem like a terrible situation to go out on Retreat, but I assure you, it isn't. You're contributing to a greater good for the sake of the Valley. For Silo's continued growth."

"But," I respond, "I want to work in neurolink. That's

why I wanted to take the class. If I get sent on Retreat, I won't be able to keep learning. I'll never become a surgeon."

Mayor Blackburn lets out a deep laugh. "Yolanda, of course you're going to have an opportunity to become a surgeon! I can't think of anyone more suited for an apprenticeship! Why in the world would you think that?"

"My sister said—"

Mayor Blackburn stops me before I can finish my thought.

"Yolanda, your sister has had a very different path from you. She's made choices that I'm sure she hasn't told you about. Made friends with some unsavory people over the years. In fact, I think having her care for you is what saved her from a very difficult life. A life"—he crouches and whispers—"that could have ended in exile."

I haven't heard that term aloud in a long time.

"I'd say *you* saved your sister from that fate."

Mayor Blackburn starts across the street.

"Walk with me," he says, ushering me. I take a few steps toward him, and he continues down Main Street. "All of this is built because of the sacrifice many of us made for a better, more connected future. Retreat is your commitment to your community. It's your sacrifice and time of reflection. When you return, you enter society ready to do what it takes for the betterment of Silo and the Greater Valley. Do you understand?"

"I think so," I say, trying to get what he's telling me.

"And Yolanda." Mayor Blackburn stops and turns. "It's better if you don't connect with the Rivera girl again. She's gotten radicalized by some unsavory ideologies that aren't good for the community."

My heart starts beating faster than I can count. He's talking about Arelis. Was he listening in on our private chats? Why would he do that? My head spins. I had a feeling something might have been wrong. I realize now she could have been trying to tell me something else on our last call. Before she disappeared. Something that had nothing to do with our TIE class.

My heart sinks into my stomach. Did she get exiled? It couldn't be. What could she have possibly done to deserve a death sentence?

I have to find her. But if she's not online, how can I reach her?

"Okay?" Mayor Blackburn says, interrupting my thoughts.

"Okay," I tell him, trying not to reveal my worry.

"Yolanda, the System helps us all stay connected as neighbors. As a community. As your mayor, it's my job to make sure I'm helping you in the best way I can. Do you understand?"

"Yes, sir."

"I'll promise you this. Once you return from Retreat,

I'll write you a personal recommendation letter myself. You'll be at the *top* of the list for any neurolink apprenticeship."

"Thank you, sir."

Mayor Blackburn laughs a little. He looks at the crowd dispersing and waves at them.

"Take care, everyone," he says, waving more before turning back to me. "I didn't get to finish my broadcast. I really wanted to share the good news with everyone in the Valley. I mean, fifty thousand credits to the *entire* Greater Valley. That's pretty good, right?"

"Really good, Mayor Blackburn. And very generous."

"Well, it's done for the good of the people. The loans just aren't working anymore. If nobody can pay, then nobody can borrow, then people get worried and stressed, and I just don't want that for our community. This money will support people so they can get what they need, plus a few little treats here and there, am I right?"

Mayor Blackburn winks and smiles. I smile back just as Cami exits the Exchange.

"Camila! I just had a wonderful conversation with Yolanda."

"Hello, Mr. Mayor," she says, kind of short.

"I was just telling her how grateful you must be for having such a talented young lady in your guardianship."

Cami looks at me, then at Mayor Blackburn. "Thank

you. Have a nice day."

Cami motions for me to follow her. I say goodbye to Mayor Blackburn and start off with Cami. She's moving her feet in short steps, like she wants to run but can't. She doesn't say anything as we cross onto Main Street.

I turn around, and Mayor Blackburn smiles and waves as we leave.

Once we're out of Silo, Cami motions for my V-probe. I know she wants to talk in private, so I don't argue with her. We pass the Sánchez farm. The autotractor isn't running. I don't see anyone in the fields. I turn my V-probe off, and Cami does the same.

"Hermana," she says with a new air of urgency, "they won't refund the scholarship money. I told them I was your guardian and hadn't signed the contract, but they said once the credits were transferred, it became binding."

"I figured," I tell her. "What about the announcement? The fifty thousand credits the mayor was offering to the Valley? We could use some of that to pay it off, can't we?"

"Like the scholarship," she tells me, "it's not that simple. We would essentially be giving up all ownership of property in exchange. It would all belong to Silo."

"I don't understand," I say, trying to figure out why that would be bad if we didn't have any more debt.

"If we give up everything we own, we can never claim anything as ours. Our home, our lives, everything will belong to Silo. That's why you read the fine print, hermana."

The sinking feeling stays inside me. I know I made a mistake, but I don't know what we can do about it now. I look toward the vast hills running along the Valley that reach the mountains in the distance. My thoughts go from having to come up with a new plan to my best friend.

"I think something happened to Arelis."

"What do you mean?"

"Mayor Blackburn talked about her being 'unsavory.' No sé; it sounded like she's in some kind of trouble."

Cami grits her teeth.

"Him and that 'unsavory' comment he loves to make. He used to say that to me all the time."

"What do you mean?"

"It's nothing," she says dismissively, and turns her V-probe back on.

There she is again. My sister not telling me anything when all I have are questions and worry. Our conversation is over. I power up my V-probe again too.

We walk the rest of the way home in relative silence. At one point, I mention what happened with Ms. Martínez and Andrés. I explain what the tech for the AIF looks like, and she tells me about Andrés's past.

"He got hurt on Retreat," she says. "He was part of an expedition searching for old computers near the edge of the Dead City."

She turns off her V-probe again and I do the same, wanting to know more. I don't know why she wants to keep everything so private, but at least she's talking. I continue to listen.

"It's very cold out there," she says. "The lake took most of the city. Then the ice came, and the city froze."

"I didn't know that had happened."

"Andrés went out there with five other kids. An entire building collapsed around them. He came back to camp alone. The whole left side of his body was broken. It's a miracle he survived. He lost his hearing. Cornelius found him a book on sign language. That's how he speaks now."

"*Another* book?"

"Yeah," she says. "That's how people used to read. Cornelius has been collecting them and leaving them as a resource for people who don't have good connectivity—or who don't want their reading habits to be *limited to one author's interpretation of everything.*"

She's talking about Hortensia Blackburn. She's written practically *every* book VOz offers. I think she's related to the mayor or something. All her stories are really loud and dramatic.

"Andrés started helping him find more books in the Dead City."

"He went back?" I say, surprised. "Even after he was almost killed?"

"For some people," she say, "the need to help others outweighs the need to just look out for themselves."

"And where do they keep the books?"

"In little huts scattered across the Outer Valley. It's like the old library systems from last century. People can check out books and return them once they are done reading them. If the System won't give people access to easy information, the books will."

"I never knew."

She stares at my V-probe. "There's a whole world out here, hermana. Not just in there."

I realize we've been offline for a while. I motion to my V-probe, and we both turn them back on. The connection light flickers on, and the System power bar displays at half connectivity.

We reach la finca, and Cami and I walk up the porch and into the house. The lights come on as we enter. She doesn't say anything when we're inside. I go to my room, and VOz powers up as soon as I enter.

"Hello, Yolanda Cicerón! Did you have a nice visit to Silo?"

There are little cameras positioned around the entire room. VOz was a gift from Silo. They wanted all citizens of the Valley to stay connected through literature. I used to stay in my room and listen to books about kids who fought dinosaurs or controlled the weather or defeated vicious animals.

I scroll through the books, and one catches my eye.

It's a children's book. Mamá used to sit with me while it played. The sound of birds. The roll of the ocean. The colors of the sky. They were meant to be peaceful images. Things appealing to a baby, like the sound of a gentle breeze or the curiosity of a grasshopper.

I press Play, and a happy tune plays in my room. A prairie meadow pops onto the screen. Then the colors show up and are highlighted as they're named.

Naranja is the color of a sunset.

Amarillo is the color of corn.

Rojo is the color of the clay in the mountain.

Plateado is the color of a precious silo.

One night, in the middle of this story, I went to grab some water in the kitchen and, from the window, saw my parents step into the fields, flick their flashlights on, and disappear into the woods. I never knew why they went or what they were looking for. A small part of me wonders if their search was connected to whatever got them exiled. But what in the world could be in those woods that warranted exiling? It doesn't make sense.

Maybe it's tied to the connection Cami made between the woods and Abuelita's work. It's possible my parents tried to read her book just like my sister did. It might be worth taking a closer look. We've tried everything else to get us out of the mess I got us into. Nothing has worked, and we're running out of practical solutions.

If the Exchange won't refund the scholarship, then maybe whatever is out there in the woods—if Cami's theory is right—might be our only option left. Even though I think it's unlikely that Abuelita's book is going to be the answer to all our problems, it's still better than having no plan at all. Might as well go see whatever the ghosts of the past hid in there—even if it might be dangerous or lead to another dead end.

I come back from my thoughts while VOz waits for my command.

"Nothing tonight, VOz," I say. "Power down."

VOz goes silent, but I know she's still listening. The System is always listening. I look at my V-probe to see if Arelis is online. There's still no sign of her. I think about Andrés and his horrible accident.

"I hope you're okay, amiga," I whisper.

Cami is out in the living room when I step outside. Her eyes are closed, so I decide not to wake her. I start for the door and it slides open. Night is falling fast. The trees cast long shadows into the woods. I step out to the yard and toward the strawberry patch. Behind the house, Abuelita's shed comes into view. It's a patchwork of metal and concrete blocks.

I never really paid much attention to this old structure.

It's on the far end of the farm, and the trees cover it from the main road cutting through the Valley. I sometimes forget it's there. I guess things can be like that. You forget them until they remind you.

The shed is padlocked. I take a few steps toward the door and fidget with the lock. Up close, the shed is rusty and worn. It looks like the buildings I saw once on a classroom virtual field trip to the coastal lands.

The buildings in those old towns are rusted and overgrown with seaweed and little snails our teacher called barnacles. I've never actually seen the ocean, but if I ever do, I bet the shed in the back of our finca will look identical to the old buildings drowned in the sea.

I move a few levers around. The lock unlatches. The door creaks open, and a musty smell wafts outside. I walk in and a light comes on. There's a workbench, and several crates are stacked against the wall. I see Abuelita's book on top of the desk. It has over five hundred pages. I stare at the title.

COLONY COLLAPSE DISORDER: A CASE FOR THE LAST BEES

by Mariela Cicerón

"Abuelita, why were you writing so much about bees?" I say, reading the author's name on the front of the book. I open the first pages and read the dedication.

To all future children—be kinder to the natural world than we were.

Along the flaps is an old picture. It must be Abuelita. Her hair is short and curly, and the colors range from gray to black to streaks of brown. She has tiny glasses on the bridge of her nose. She's smiling, and her head is slightly tilted and leaning into a redbrick wall.

She has the biggest, roundest, most beautiful dark brown eyes I have ever seen.

A surge runs through me. It's an unexplainable feeling inside. I stare at her face for a while and find myself smiling back at her. Like I've known her my whole life.

There's more information about Abuela printed on the back of the book.

Mariela García Cicerón, PhD

School of Life and Environmental Sciences—Advanced Technology Division

Havana Institute of Agriculture

"Abuela was a doctor!" I blurt out. The light flickers on and off. The shed door pushes open and closed. A gust of wind shoots inside. The book drops and thuds on the floor.

"Hello?" I say, watching the setting sun inch into the room. I scoop the book up and carefully make my way toward the door. Is there someone outside? The wind sweeps in again, causing the door to swing back and forth.

I hear the faint sound of grasshoppers and little night birds starting their evening calls.

"Don't be silly, Yoly," I tell myself. "It's just the wind."

The sun highlights the strawberry patch and the trees along the farm. I look at the book again. The portrayal of bees in VOz doesn't seem the same as the bees Abuelita is writing about. She wanted the future children of the world to be kinder to the earth. Somehow the bees and their collapse are a part of that, though I don't understand how yet. There are scientific descriptions of trees and strange names of flora and fauna. Then there are details about the bees' genetic makeup and in-depth descriptions of their bodies. It's all written very pragmatically. There isn't a lot of narration. Just facts and figures. I understand the language she's writing in—it's the language of science. The details of how and why things work the way they do.

I keep reading through the dense writing. No wonder Cami wanted me to look at it. This is exactly the kind of research-heavy reading material I love to learn about!

I look out the door again.

"Why didn't you ever show this to me, Cami?" I say in the quiet of the shed.

I land on a page with a photograph and some more information.

A structure of waxy hexagonal cells produced by Apis mellifera *where their young are reared and the viscous food substance is made. Genus and substance highly sanative.*

It looks like a comb of some kind. Then I notice the substance. It's amber colored. It looks like the liquid inside the jar that woman was carrying yesterday. The lady coming out of the mayor's mansion. She was telling him they needed to find more. Maybe this substance and the one the lady was carrying is the same.

I keep reading. Abuelita describes the hive these insects build. The details on the flora and fauna are scattered across the page. It's hard to decipher all the unfamiliar words. I can see why Cami had so much trouble. But there's enough information to understand that whatever Abuelita was writing about, the answers seem to be pointing to the woods.

I close the book, step outside of the shed, and scan the woods.

"What did you leave in there, Abuelita?" I say, hoping to find something, anything that can pay off my scholarship and avoid me having to serve time on Retreat.

There's an entrance into the woods in between two large oaks. I can hardly see the darkening sky under the canopy of the trees. I check my V-probe. It'll be nighttime in about an hour. I step over a few exposed roots and pause. My V-probe blinks melodically. I place it on a rock near the entrance to the woods.

"In case I lose connection in there. Don't want an

infraction on top of everything else."

There's a slope ahead. I grab a branch and carefully slide down. The trees get denser the farther I get into the woods. They completely blanket the sky. After about twenty minutes of walking, I realize I've gone completely off the path.

CHAPTER 8

Nature Calls

The woods are peaceful but also unsettling. I've been walking for what seems like hours. Every tree looks exactly like the other. At one point I'm pretty sure I go around the same tree stump for the tenth time.

Abuelita's book is still in my hand. I look at the cover again. The pages are full of photographs of bees hovering around flowers, making something called honey and then a pesticide was sprayed that slowly killed them off.

"Neonicotinoids," I say, reading the description.

I keep looking around for a sign. Anything that could clue me in as to why my family has been so obsessed with these woods. I'm absolutely sure it has something to do with the bees now, but I'm not sure what it is. Maybe it's an old pot of money Abuelita stashed away for safekeeping and is guarded by killer bees that only her notes can protect us from!

Nah, that would be ridiculous. Besides, Abuelita talks about the bees' decline and their extinction. Like how humans dumped pesticides on them and killed them off. I doubt she has a secret army of monster bees protecting her treasure.

I hear a rustling up ahead and drop my book in surprise. "Chiquita, is that you?" I call out nervously.

A pair of glowing eyes shine from the bush, followed by the spotted furry head and large round belly. Chiquita pops out from the bushes and laughs as she moves gingerly toward me.

"You okay?" I ask her as she crouches and starts licking her hind leg. I notice she has a large metal shard near her tail. "What happened to you?"

There are snapped branches and scattered leaves. There seems to have been a fight of some kind. I notice a shiny object on the ground. It looks like a claw. Kind of like the ones on the AIF drones I saw earlier.

"What in the world did you get into a fight with, Chiquita?"

I approach carefully.

Chiquita turns her snout toward my outstretched hand, her two bottom teeth jutting into the sides of her nose. If she decided to attack, I wouldn't stand a chance. I pull my hand away.

"Um, I'll get Cami to help you," I say while Chiquita starts rubbing against my leg. She laughs and grunts a few more times. I know she probably isn't going to hurt me. But she's a wild animal. She could get mad if I pull that thing out of her leg.

"Are you going to bite my arm off if I help you?"

Chiquita watches me. She looks uncomfortable. I should at least try to help her.

"Okay," I tell her, inching toward the metal shard. "But if you do, I'm going to be really mad!"

I carefully reach my hand toward her head and slowly move it along the side of her whiskers and behind her ears. She closes her eyes and purrs. I rub her ears more, and she nuzzles into my arm.

"It's okay," I comfort her. I reach down her long back and rub her belly. She sits on her side, and the shard sticks out from her hind leg. Her coarse fur meets the sharp metal. The cold steel pressed into her skin is a reminder of how different the two things are. One is a manufactured thing, cold and lifeless. The other is a living, breathing thing. My other hand goes onto Chiquita's belly. Through her breathing I can feel her heartbeat.

"Easy, girl," I say as my hand moves over the metal shard. "One, two—"

On three I quickly pull the shard out. Chiquita rolls and growls and springs up.

"Whoa," I say, getting up and moving back as Chiquita hunches over like she's going to pounce. "It's out," I tell her, showing her the shard. "See?"

I throw the metal on the ground, and Chiquita watches it roll around into a patch of shrubs. She looks back at me, then starts licking her hind leg. She makes that low guttural laugh again, then disappears back into the woods.

"You're welcome!" I call out, but before I can track where she's gone, Chiquita is already out of sight. A surge of pride rushes over me as I walk back to Abuelita's book and scoop it up in my hands.

"See that, Abuelita?" I say. "Doctor Yoly to the rescue!"

Some light breaks through the trees. The sun hasn't disappeared just yet, so I can see enough to move but not enough to know exactly where I'm going. Our forest is bigger than I remember. There are drops and mounds and rocks littered throughout the area.

I climb up on a boulder and look out. There is a drop before I can get to more ground. I jump off the boulder and land in a wet, marshy patch of mud.

"Great." I look at the globs of wet dirt caked on my boots. "That's never going to come off."

I shake my leg and try to get some of the mud off my boot. It just slides lazily to the outer soles and barely falls to the ground. The mud doesn't want to go anywhere but instead stays, messing up the only pair of boots I own.

Inspecting the area, I can see it's a mostly dried-up stream. It follows a natural route. I wonder if the stream leads all the way back to la finca. I realize it's getting late, and I'm tired. I don't want to get more lost than I already am, so I decide to find my way home. No wonder my parents and Cami never found anything. These woods are enormous! I avoid squishing in more mud while I try to walk back.

"Chiquita will be okay," I keep telling myself. "She's a wild animal; they know how to defend themselves out here."

A large branch lies across the dried-up stream like a bridge. I step across and knock on the tree on the other side. It sounds hollow. The bark peels off easily. The branch is rotting inside. The ground looks moist like the stream, but there's a strange smell to it. Like whatever is in the ground isn't meant to be there. This tree must be dying.

I notice a perimeter of shrubs with bright yellow flowers on them. It looks like a fence. Almost like a tiny forest within a forest surrounding what looks like a collection of large stones. This isn't the way I came.

I step through the small opening to see if there's another way to get back up the small ledge. The temperature suddenly drops the moment I walk through.

"How can the air be so cool in here?" I say to myself. The rocks and stones feel cool as well.

"It's like the temperature is controlled by the placement of the trees and the stones."

There's a large tree at the far end of the circle. It rises high above the rest of the smaller ones that wrap around the collection of rocks. Another little shrub rests near the stones. It looks more like a canopy of twisted weeds than an actual shrub. Like a hut of some kind. It's covering a small hole. I peel away the weeds and move the branches over.

"What the—?"

I place Abuelita's book down by my feet and inspect. A winged yellow insect is curled into a ball. When I inspect it further, I see it has a stinger and two large bulgy eyes and looks like the awful bees from *The Scourge*. It's lying next to the small hole.

"Okay, Abuelita," I say, hoping the insect isn't alive. "I trust you," I say, looking at the bee on the book's cover. I step closer.

I move a small stick toward the bee and turn it over. How can this thing still be here? Wouldn't it have decomposed or something? It has fuzz on its back like the pollinator drones.

"This definitely isn't tech."

I look more closely to see how it's curled up on the

ground. There's a little pointer at the end of its tail. Dark yellow colors make up the bee's body. Its eyes are black, and the antennae are folded over its round head. I pick the little creature up. It covers barely an inch of my hand. The fuzzy body tickles my palm when I roll it around. It starts to twitch. Before I can react, its body stiffens and the little pointer on its tail whips down into my palm and pricks it.

"Owww!"

I toss the wiggling creature to the ground. It twitches around on the dirt and then goes still. On my palm a tiny little pointer sticks out of my skin.

"What did you do that for?!"

I carefully pull the stinger out and examine my hand. I move out of the shrub and stumble back. A branch juts out and scratches my leg. I twist around and my ankle gets stuck. When I fall, I feel something snap. A sharp pain shoots up my leg and into my stomach. I go dizzy. My ankle throbs. It instantly swells up. I clasp at my foot, but it hurts too much. The sting momentarily escapes, and all I can think about is the pain in my ankle.

This is why I don't venture into the woods! Or spend time outside! The pain continues rising and squeezing so tight my entire leg is going to explode.

The tree next to me acts as a support as I try to get up. I move out of the cool air surrounded by small trees and back into the rest of the forest. I find the creek and hope the clearer path south leads back to la finca.

I don't know what hurts more, the sting or my likely broken ankle. Each step feels like a thousand rocks are rubbing against my foot. I grab branches all the way back home, trying my best to not fall. My mouth is dry and I'm getting dizzy. I keep looking at my hand and thinking about that gruesome insect sting in *The Scourge*.

"Please don't explode," I say, thinking the bee that just stung me looks just like the one that stung the guy's hand in the book. "Please don't explode!"

I try to reassure myself that Abuelita wouldn't want to protect something that would make my limb explode. Also, I realize that VOz seems to exaggerate for dramatic effect, so maybe it's not as bad as it appears. Still, it hurts *a lot* and I need to get home!

I walk and stumble in the darkness of the woods for what feels like hours until I finally reach the dirt road just outside the entrance to the forest. I manage to look up and see Cami running toward me.

"Yoly, what are you doing out in the woods at night?"

"Not now, Cami! My hand! It might explode!"

"Pero, ¿qué pasó? Are you okay? And why are you limping? What happened?!"

I don't have time to answer Cami's thirty questions. I'm in too much pain.

"I need . . . I need to check out my ankle," I say, trying

to get the words out. "And . . . and my hand. I got stung!"

"Stung? By what?"

Cami takes my hand and wraps her arm around me. She takes weight off my ankle and helps me into the house.

"What could you have possibly been doing out there at this hour, Yoly?"

"I was—" I say, trying to control the pain. "I was in the shed, and I started reading Abuelita's book, and you were sleeping, and I just went in—"

"You just went in?" Cami says, digging around for bandages. "What in the world could you be looking for in the woods before nighttime?"

"You said Abuelita . . . Abuelita's book and the woods," I hedge, not sure where Cami's V-probe might be.

I close my eyes and try not to think about the pain while my sister looks for bandages. Suddenly, I sit up straight.

"The book! Cami, I left the book in the woods!"

"Yoly," Cami says, returning to my side with wraps and a cold pack. She feels around my ankle and presses down around the bones. "It's just a sprain."

My sister starts wrapping my ankle. A worried look comes across her face. "Going out in the woods by yourself at night is not a good idea. I mean, you're hurt!"

"I'm sorry," I say. "It wasn't nighttime when I left. I just thought, the book—" I can't get any more words out. Cami puts the cold pack on my ankle and then ties the bandage in place. The cooling eases the pain.

"I was worried about you," she says, caressing my hair. She holds my face, giving it a gentle squeeze, then takes my hand and rubs my palm.

"Ow!" A sting runs up my thumb, and I pull my hand away. Cami inspects my hand. There's a slight reddish swell at the center of my palm. I keep waiting for it to puff up, but it doesn't. It just burns a little.

After a moment, her eyes go wide.

"Yoly," she says, whispering so quietly I can hardly hear. "What stung you?"

"I found one," I say, but she hushes me.

"Sh, sh, not here," she quiets. Cami helps me outside, and I tell her the whole story.

CHAPTER 9

FN

We leave Cami's V-probe behind and go inside the shed. My sister listens as I tell her about the substance I discovered in Abuelita's book.

"I think the bees make it," I tell her. "I saw a lady with Mayor Blackburn carrying a jar similar to the liquid in Abuelita's book."

"She's his sister," she says, still looking distracted. "Her name is Hortensia."

"The author?"

Cami nods.

"I—" She pauses like she wants to say something but can't. "I worked for her."

"Doing what?"

"Mostly cleaning and washing and things like that. I found something once," she admits. "It was the same jar you saw. She quickly hid it from me. Called me a thief. Said I was trying to rob her. After that, I—" She stops herself.

I feel my palms get sweaty and my breath shorten.

"You got sent on Retreat," I say quietly.

Cami nods.

All this time never knowing why Cami was sent away, and it was all because she was falsely accused. My sister is annoying, like, super pesada most of the time, but I know she's not a thief. She would never take anything that didn't belong to her. Why would Hortensia frame her like that?

"I wish you would've told me—"

"It's not important," she interrupts. "What matters is getting you out of that scholarship. If we could find some honey of our own"—she points to my palm—"we might be able to trade for your scholarship money."

"No, wait, Cami; this is important! *Why* didn't you ever tell me? Why do you always hide things from me?"

Cami doesn't say anything. She looks around, then moves outside. I follow her.

"I . . . I made a promise—"

She stops herself from continuing.

"To who? Mamá y Papá?" I push.

Cami doesn't say a word. She just looks around like she's

worried about something.

"You start sharing a little; then you go and close up on me all over again. You're not the only one who lost Mamá y Papá, Cami. I did too! And it wouldn't be so lonely without them if my sister would actually share things with me. Are you going to *ever* talk to me, hermana, or are you just going to leave little fragments like some giant code for me to map out?"

My sister leaves for the house without another word.

"Ahhh!" I yell so loud my voice carries across the field.

My V-probe is still on the rock near the edge of the woods. It's the longest I've ever been without it. To be honest, I haven't even thought about it. It makes a strange beeping sound. It's dark, but the V-probe's beeps help me easily find it.

When I reach the rock, I notice it flashing strange codes.

"What's going on with you?" I say, scooping it up.

The signal flickers. A polar bear avatar flashes on the screen, then disappears.

"Arelis?"

I scan the V-probe, but it doesn't let me connect. The polar bear pops up again.

"Arelis!"

I try to connect, but my keyboard is disabled.

"What the—?"

It flickers on and off. Then a message runs across the screen.

FREE NETWORK ACCESS: GRANTED

The polar bear shoots back onto the screen. It salutes, then disappears again. My V-probe goes dark, then powers up again. The System icon appears on the screen.

SYSTEM REBOOT IN PROCESS

My V-probe syncs back online. The double *S* symbol identifying the Silo System appears on my screen. The home page comes back to my V-probe, and all my applications show up on my screen. My scholarship note is in the upper corner. My neurolink class flashes an assignment due tomorrow morning. Everything looks normal until I notice a small icon at the bottom of the screen.

"FN?" I squint to read. I look around.

Cami is already back inside. I hear only the grasshoppers, the night birds, and the quiet electrical hum of my screen as I stand at the edge of the woods and wonder what in the world just happened with my V-probe. Did it get hacked? Whatever it was, I'm not telling Cami. Two can play the keeping-things-from-your-sister game.

I need to figure out what the appearance of Arelis's avatar meant. I'm not sure what the Free Network is either or how it accessed my V-probe, but I know Arelis was there.

She was trying to communicate.

I pace around my room, trying to piece it together. After a few hours, I open my door and see Cami has gone to sleep.

Maybe I should tell her about Arelis's message, but then she would probably just tell me to ignore it for my own safety. I wish I could get her to see that I can handle myself and whatever truth she feels compelled to keep from me. I know I made a mistake with the scholarship, but I can help. I just want her to see that.

I look around my room and at VOz's cameras on all four corners of my walls. When we log in to the System, we never ask who gets to see what we're doing or who we're talking to. My sister has always been wary of the System, but she's been even more cautious lately. I keep looking at the VOz cameras.

Maybe she isn't keeping secrets from me but from the devices listening all around us. The mayor seemed overly concerned about my friendship with Arelis. So much so that he felt he had to listen to our chat. How many times has he done that? The thought makes my skin crawl.

I look at my palm. It's still a little red, but the swelling has gone down. Cami might feel safer talking in the woods, away from all this technology. No V-probes to turn on and off every five minutes. If I show her where I found the bee, maybe the secrets she's keeping will finally start to reveal themselves.

My V-probe screen lights up again. The little FN link gives a gentle glow like it's breathing. I click on the icon. It goes dark, and then a message flashes across the screen. It looks like programming code, but instead of zeroes and ones, there are words.

SY<>FN. Panda. Bro. SI.ToC. Plsassist

The screen goes blank again.

The FN icon stops blinking. It doesn't respond when I click on it again.

Arelis, what are you trying to say?

I try to decode the meaning by mapping out the letters in the message.

Panda. She was calling me. Bro. Something about Cornelius. I don't know the middle part. *Plsassist.* Please assist!

I look up from my screen. The walls are blank, but I know VOz is listening. Arelis needs my help. Her brother is in trouble.

CHAPTER 10
Las Últimas Apicultoras

The next morning before going back into the woods, I ask Cami to go with me and she agrees. Like she knows I want to talk in private. After a light breakfast, I log in to class. As I enter the room, Dr. Sime is giving a test on brain tissue and cerebral cortex functions. I take my seat and stare at the questions appearing on my desk. Half the questions are written in Latin. I know only a little Latin, because some phrases look like words in Spanish. I do my best to answer, and after about an hour, I finally turn in the test.

Dr. Sime grades it right in front of me and hands it back. I totally failed.

"I never got a message we were going to have an exam, Dr. Sime," I say. "Only that we had homework. And I couldn't understand some of the questions, because they were written in Latin."

"Amat victoria curam," he says.

"*Victoria* probably means 'victory' and *curar* means 'to cure' in Spanish," I say. "It means victory cures all."

"It means 'victory likes preparation' but yes, victory *does* indeed cure all. Latin is the language of medicine and science, YOLA012108."

"No other languages practiced medicine before?" I answer back.

I hear a few giggles from the class. Dr. Sime doesn't seem impressed.

"If you fail again," he says, "you will be removed from the class without refund, YOLA012108. Intellegisne quod tibi dicam?"

"Yes," I tell him, figuring out what he's saying. "I understand perfectly."

When class is over, I log out of school. I make a note on my V-probe to read up on Latin. I step out toward the living room, and Cami is already waiting.

"How's the ankle feel?"

"It's fine. The anti-inflammatory wraps worked. What's in the bag?"

"Things for our walk," she says.

We go outside, and Cami places the duffel down and activates the hover feature. The duffel rises, and Cami fastens the band around her wrist, commanding the bag to follow us.

"Did you take Latin when you were in school?" I ask while we walk to the woods.

"No," she says, moving to the path inside. "Abuelita hablaba conmigo en español," she tells me.

"Mamá y Papá combined English and Spanish. People in Silo mostly speak English," I say.

"¿Por qué preguntas?"

"Dr. Sime started speaking Latin in class. Said it was the language of medicine and science."

"He sounds obnoxious."

Cami steps through the two trees. "I never liked the way they taught subjects," she says before going farther inside. "They want this throwback to some great time before it turned bad. But like with everything else, they ignore all the ways things today are worse than ever."

"How do you mean?" I ask.

Cami places her V-probe near the edge of the woods. I check my own and see the little FN icon. I want to stay connected in case Arelis reaches out, but my sister seems to finally want to talk. I don't want to lose my chance. I place my V-probe down next to hers and walk after her. Cami continues.

"They send kids out to the Dead City to pick up scraps and cables and files to *retrofit* them with new life. They make it impossible to pay things back because whenever you think you can pay back the debt, something breaks down and you take out another loan to fix the problem. It never ends. And now they've got these *scholarships*, which basically make you pay back your education by doing free labor."

Cami walks like she's lost in thought. The leaves on the ground crunch as she steps, and the wind picks up around us, bringing humid air into the woods.

"I'm sorry about last night, Yoly. I *do* want to share with you more. And I know you're not a little girl anymore."

She pauses and looks at me with this strange smile.

"Even though I still remember you with that curly little puff of hair and those baggy little frocks you used to run around in, making mud pies and pretending to eat them. ¡Qué linda!"

She tries to pinch my cheek, but I immediately pull away and stare at her.

"Please don't," I say, staring. "And don't ever tell that story to anyone, *ever*."

Cami laughs, then sighs like she's letting out a breath she's been holding in for a long time.

"I think part of it was that *I* wasn't ready to talk about them or anything from the past for the longest time," she admits. "You were only six when I returned. Mamá y Papá, they told me to take care of you. To—" She stops herself.

"To what, Cami?"

"To not tell you anything about these woods or Abuelita's work, or anything that could put you in danger. They made me promise."

"But why? Why would they do that?"

"To keep you safe."

She reaches into her pocket and pulls out a paper.

"Mamá asked me to give this to you when you were old enough, to explain everything," she says, handing me the paper. "I didn't know if you were ready. But you've been ready for a long time, haven't you? I'm sorry for not seeing that sooner."

I unfold it and see it's written in ink, like Abuela's journal. The letter is addressed to me. After looking it over a few times, I start to understand the words:

> Mi querida Yolanda,
>
> We put a great burden on you and your sister, but it was the only way to keep you both safe. Abuelita's book will guide you both. Lean on each other, and find allies in the community, and don't lose the forest for the trees. Trust the bees. They are your guides. The burden is yours now, like it was mine, and your abuelita's before. You are both las últimas apicultoras.
>
> Love always,
>
> Mamá

I look up at Cami. We both stare at each other.

"I kept the letter stored away in my room. Hidden from Mayor Blackburn, from everyone in Silo, from—"

"Me," I finish.

Cami looks down.

"I grabbed the letter this morning and decided it was long overdue I shared it with you."

"Did she write you one too?"

"No, she didn't have time," Cami admits, her lips shaking a little as she talks. "That machine grabbed her," she says between breaths, "but she yanked away and rushed over to me. Pulled me in close."

"What did she say?"

"She told me to protect you at all costs," she says, starting to tear up. My sister has been keeping in so much for so long. It's like a valve is releasing after years and years of sealed-in air pressure. "She said to keep you safe by keeping your curiosity centered on your schooling. She talked about how bright you were. Always asking questions. Trying to figure why things are the way they are."

Warm pools stream down my face. My sister continues.

"But she said that curiosity at such a young age will get you in trouble in this world, hermana. She wanted me to keep you safe until you were old enough to use that curiosity for a greater purpose. Then that thing clamped on and pried her away from me. Papá tried to step in and help, but it just grabbed him too. Dragged them off and threw them in the SDV truck." Cami wipes her face and collects herself. "But maybe that was the wrong thing to do. I should have given you tools so you could protect yourself. I should have told you."

"You did what she asked, Cami," I say, coming in close, not wanting to be angry with my sister when she's sharing so much. But a part of me is upset. I could have understood so much more if she would have given me the letter sooner. I try to push the thought away. I can't be mad at her for doing what she thought was right. "You're telling me now, hermana," I say, trying to comfort her. Cami wipes the last tears from her face.

"That thing ripped her away," she says, anger forming in her voice. "She and Papá were exiled. For what?" I watch my sister as she clenches her jaw and balls her hands into fists. "They took them from us and never explained why. Now we're left with these shattered pieces scattered everywhere and no understanding of how to put them back together again."

I look at the trees surrounding us. My sister, a combination of sadness and anger. My mother and father paid a price for something that they did or found in these woods. The bees.

"I'm good at putting things together, hermana," I tell her, mapping out the details in Mamá's letter. "And you're good at keeping us together, and safe."

My sister nods.

"Maybe we're the ones to break the cycle," I tell her, thinking about Abuelita's book, about the bees, and about my parents. About everything.

"Yeah," my sister says, nodding.

I continue to look at Cami and watch the mix of sadness and anger blend into a face of hope and determination. Maybe my mother wanted to keep me safe until the time came for our journey into the woods to reveal what we really must do. My thoughts go back to Mamá's letter.

My sister was sent on Retreat because she was wrongly accused of stealing. And at seventeen, she was asked to take care of her little sister. I never understood why Cami acted the way she did. I do now. She's never had a choice. It's always been forced on her.

"I wish she was here to tell you all this," Cami adds. "I don't know exactly why they were exiled or what our *burden* truly is, but I do know that it all has something to do with these woods and the bees inside them."

"My thoughts exactly, hermana."

Cami offers a smile.

"I'm sorry that I'm a poor substitute for Mamá," she says. "The last thing I want is for you to feel alone. Even when it hurt to talk about them, I should have been willing for you, Yoly."

"I'm sorry you've had to carry this alone, Cami," I tell her, taking her hand. Her metallic fingers wrap around mine. I rub her shoulder and bring her into my arms. We stay there in the warmth of our embrace, and it's the safest I've felt in my whole life.

"I promise you that I'll tell you everything I know now," she says, her face sagging a little again. She's been holding so much for so long. It makes me sad for her and me.

"No more secrets, okay?" I tell her. "I want to know what happened to you too."

She takes a breath, then begins as we keep walking.

"When I was fourteen," Cami starts, "you were a baby—barely two years old. Abuelita had already . . ." She pauses, not wanting to finish. I plead with her to continue.

"Mamá called you a miracle. And you were"—my sister smiles—"you really were a miracle. Times were tough that year. Crops were dying all over the Valley. We hadn't produced any fruit the entire season. One market day, I saw Papá talking to Mayor Blackburn. Then Mamá left our stand and went to the Exchange. They took out a loan. But things didn't get better. We didn't have much food, and even though people around the Valley tried to help each other, it was still hard. The community in the Valley comes together, but if everyone is down, there isn't much we can do to bring each other up. Except maybe hope things will turn around."

I listen closely to every word Cami says.

"I went into Silo and looked for work. I thought maybe I could earn some money and help out. I worked hauling used parts to Silo, sold old tech on the markets. Even tried working in the factory floor rebuilding and retrofitting old machinery. But I never made enough money. I was making just enough to help with the minimum debt payments."

"You were only fourteen," I say, thinking how she was just two years older than I am now when she was out there working, trying to help our family.

"Yeah," she continues. "Then Mayor Blackburn offered me a job. I would clean his house and tend to his sister's needs."

"Hortensia," I say, and Cami nods.

"She's a strange lady," she says. "Calls herself 'the author of over fifty books for adults and children.' Always asked me about Abuelita. Seemed obsessed with knowing *everything* about her. I trusted her. Told her what I knew. Some stuff about bees. Other stuff about honey. I didn't know any better. Then one day, I was dusting her closet and found the jar. She saw me and told Mayor Blackburn I was trying to steal it. All he said was, 'I'm disappointed you've become such an unsavory citizen of the Valley, Miss Cicerón. I don't know what we're going to do with you.'"

"So, he sent you on Retreat without giving you a chance

to explain yourself?" I say, thinking how Mayor Blackburn acts like he wants to help but really just seems to be doing things that just make people rely on him and nobody else. I start running through all the times he offered to "help."

"No, *he* didn't send me on Retreat," she says, lost in thought. "I was sent home. A few days later, our power goes off. The Exchange showed up demanding payment or we were going to lose the farm. Mayor Blackburn made an offer. He negotiated with the Exchange people and said our debt could not be forgiven but we could keep the farm if I went on Retreat for two years. Up to that point, only volunteers went on Retreat. And there weren't that many."

"No, hermana," I say, feeling my palms get sweaty.

"When I reported to training, I saw dozens of kids from the Valley. They called us the first 'repayment team.' We were the first to go on Retreat in exchange for the debt our families owed. Most of us didn't survive. It was so cold. There's no power. Decaying buildings have a way of collapsing at any moment."

"Like what happened to Andrés?"

Cami nods.

"Two years later, they sent me home. Saying the debt had been paid. I didn't understand. When I came back, Mamá y Papá were being taken away."

I can see the weight of the world behind Cami's eyes. Like they've seen and felt and experienced more than anyone her age should ever have to experience.

"Mamá slipped the letter in my pocket," she says. "Once they left in that SDV, I knew we wouldn't ever see them again."

Everything Cami tells me drowns my thoughts.

"I've gone into these woods every day for the last six years," she continues, "looking for some clue. Something they might have left behind to guide us. But I never got far. I was worried if something happened to me out here, you'd be left alone. I went to Abuelita's shed and couldn't understand the book in its entirety. Abuelita used really technical language!"

I laugh.

"I love that kind of writing."

"That's why you figured it out so quickly!"

My sister and I smile at each other.

"It's nice talking to you," she says.

"Yeah," I tell her, feeling a rush of emotion.

As we go farther into the woods, I scan for the muddy, mostly dried-out creek.

"Do you remember where you found the bee?"

"It was about a thirty-minute walk from here," I tell her. "There was a little hole and a circle of small shrubs with stones and rocks in the middle. Once you walk inside, the temperature drops to like sixty degrees."

"Do you remember how to get there from here?"

"There's a dried-out creek," I say. "You can't see it from the edge of the woods, but after about a mile it starts to get muddy and wet. We can follow that to the circle of little bushes."

"Okay," she says.

"We should look for Chiquita too," I tell her. "I want to see how she's doing."

"So, you care about her, huh?"

"I mean, she stinks like wet fur and she has giant teeth and could eat me alive, but sure, I guess she's okay."

My sister raises an eyebrow. "Right," she says sarcastically as we carefully step over fallen branches and walk deeper into the forest. I spot the creek, and we make our way along its dried-out path. After hiking for about twenty minutes, we approach the fallen branch making a bridge across the waterless creek.

"It was around here," I say, stepping over a few branches.

We approach the tree, and I show Cami the rotted branch. Up ahead I catch sight of the little shrub of vines. When we enter the circle of small shrubs, Cami comments on the sudden temperature change.

"Amazing," she marvels. "It's humid everywhere else but here."

"Yeah," I tell her, feeling the chill. "There it is!" I point to the shrub with vines and weeds.

We inspect the site, and I notice copper wires placed

around the shrubs. Abuelita's book is lying on the ground. I pick it up. I'm relieved it isn't wet or damaged. The bee isn't around the bushes. It's gone.

"Where did it go?" I say, looking around. "I swear it was here!"

"I believe you," she says, digging around looking for clues.

I look around, then stop and stare.

"Cami," I say, watching the tall tree in front of us. "Look."

There's a massive hole in the tree. I open Abuelita's book and find the page about bees living in trees. Cami looks at the page; then we both stare at the tree.

About thirty feet in the air, shielded by lush leaves and twisting branches, an entire hive of bees hovers in and out of the nest. From where we stand, we can hardly see them. They're almost camouflaged.

"It's a hive," Cami says. "Yoly, you found it."

"Look," I say, checking out the little hole in the middle of the shrub. "It's like a tunnel of some kind."

Two more bees crawl out of the hole and buzz up to the tree. There seems to be a network between the hole in the ground and the hive in the tree.

"Mira." Cami points to the tree. A rich, dark, gooey substance is dripping from a slit in the tree. "It's honey, Yoly."

The thick liquid drips slowly down the side of the tree. We both stand in silence as the dark golden substance mesmerizes us. I find a page in Abuelita's book about extraction.

"Her notes explain everything," I say, scanning the book. "How to extract it, how to remove it from this thing called a comb, and look." I show her detailed instructions about bottling the honey from a hive in a tree.

"Hermana," Cami says, reading. "We just bought your scholarship."

"You really think Hortensia will buy it from us?"

"She'll definitely buy it, Yoly," Cami says.

My sister and I marvel at the honey dripping from the bark. I think about Arelis's encrypted note. Maybe this honey can help her and Cornelius as well? The bees buzz lazily around the hive. The golden substance could be the answer to all our problems.

We watch the bees floating in the air for a while. Something my mom said in her letter sticks with me. She called my sister and me *las últimas apicultoras*. I may not know much Latin, but I know Spanish. Mamá called us—the Last Beekeepers.

CHAPTER 11

The Fog of Memory

I decide to tell Cami about Arelis's message on our walk home from the hive.

"She figured out a way to communicate outside of the System," I tell her.

"It's dangerous, Yoly," she cautions. "Mayor Blackburn has his ears *everywhere*. And we don't know anything about this new system. For all we know it could be the mayor trying to trick us."

"It's not," I tell my sister. "I know Arelis. I know I should have told you about it earlier, and I know I messed up with the scholarship, but we can't abandon our friends, Cami."

Cami knows I'm right. Even though she's worried, she

understands we need to find a way to help.

"Fine," she says. "But the moment I suspect something is off, we shut it down."

"Deal," I say.

We don't have time to say anything else as we get closer to the entrance of the woods and the spot where we placed our V-probes. We kept them on while we left to not raise any flags of inactivity, and when I pick mine up again, I'm glad to see no warning signs are flashing across the screen.

I notice the little FN icon gives off a slight pulse again. I open it and see there's a response function to Arelis's last message. It's not very advanced, but the fact that she created something to communicate outside of the System chat functions is absolutely incredible. I press her message, and a response line appears below it. I can't type full sentences. There seems to be a character limit of some kind.

Hola, Polar Bear. Panda found a way. Meet?

"I hope she gets it," I say to Cami.

"Sh, sh," she hushes, then points to the V-probe, and I don't disagree. Something inside is telling me we should be even more careful now that we've discovered the beehive.

We both use the V-probes to show activity, then leave them near the trees to explore Abuelita's shed. We dig around looking for other little secrets Abuelita must have left in here. It's amazing how something can be right in front of you for so long and you never realize all the things you can discover from it.

"Hey," Cami says, carrying a metal tube with a handle.

"What is that?"

"I have no idea," Cami says, reading Abuelita's journal. "There's a picture that looks just like this," she says, showing me Abuelita's picture. Cami reads the description. "It says it's a 'smoker.'"

"Why would Abuela need a smoker?"

"Not sure," Cami says, checking out some of the mechanisms, then referencing Abuelita's journal.

I look up and see copper wires covering the ceiling.

"Cami, look." I point. "That's the same metal that was on the rocks by the hive. It was hidden in between the stones around the bushes."

I wonder why there would be copper wires here and back in the woods where the beehive was. I flip the pages of her book and try to find some clues. They are mostly chapters dedicated to different species of bees and the environments they inhabited.

The space where the beehive is seems like it was intentionally set up that way. The copper wires around the stones and the bushes would have had to have been placed there on purpose. Why would Abuelita do that?

I close the book and look at the flap. It looks like all her accomplishments are listed next to her picture. She won a whole bunch of awards for her research on bee decline. But it doesn't say anything about tending to bees.

"There's nothing in the book about caring for them. Only bottling honey," I say while Cami tries to fit a canister to the smoker. "Cami, *why* are you playing with that thing?"

"Because I think it's supposed to be used with the bees."

"To what? Burn them?"

"No, Yoly!" she says. "These boxes have liners that look like the hive on the tree. And the smoker was right next to these old crates. I think it has something to do with moving the bees in here."

I pick up Abuelita's book. Nothing in there seems like an exaggeration. It's presenting facts and figures. Information. *The Scourge* reads a lot differently. Cami continues to work on the smoker and references Abuelita's journal for directions. I turn back to the desk and keep reading. There's a section about the honey that bees produce. There's nothing like this in Silo. We could sell this in town for a lot of money. Not just to Hortensia.

Cami continues to look through Abuelita's shed while I read her book. It's hundreds of pages long. There are drawings and charts of various species of bees. There is a wide range of beekeeping measures and honey-harvesting methods that help explain some of the drawings in Abuel-ita's journal.

My head and my heart are a jumble of emotions and thoughts. For years I've waited for Cami to talk to me about our family, about her, about the farm for more than a minute at a time. And in one day, I know more about my sister than I've ever known.

It makes me think about all those times I was mad at her for telling me to be quiet when I was asking questions. All those times she would tell me to not go into Abuelita's shed or venture out into the woods or talk to too many people in Silo. She was just doing what Mamá had asked her to do. She was being a good daughter. A good sister.

I'm grateful to her for finally sharing, but I think I'm also frustrated. If I had known all this, I wouldn't have accepted the scholarship. I wouldn't have felt so alone all the time. Isolated from everyone that Cami thought could be dangerous. I understand why Mamá was worried, but keeping things from me only made her worst fears come true. Now I'm in debt, and I might get sent on Retreat like Cami. I don't want to be mad at my sister though. Not anymore. She's been through so much.

I look at Cami and see how happy she is talking so openly with me. Like she's free of the burden of having to keep things from her sister for so long. I turn back to look at Abuelita's book and read a few pages.

"I found it!" I say, flagging the page. "There are guidelines to tending the bees and detailed descriptions about the science behind the upkeep of the hive."

"Well, you're the science- and tech-minded one," Cami says.

"And you like getting your hands dirty," I respond, pointing to the journal.

"I guess so."

I skim through more pages and read more chapters. There is a system on how to prep before going out to the hive. A notation about tending to the drone bees and several pages dedicated to the queen bee. The queen runs the whole hive. Every bee in the colony follows her lead. I skim a few more pages.

There's a section on bee extraction. It details the safe removal of the bees from their trees and into the crates, where they will be free from pesticides and harmful insects.

I notice a picture of a giant-looking bee on one of the pages. It says:

Vespa mandarinia—*a giant wasp species. Highly invasive. Can destroy entire bee colony.*

I continue reading.

"The giant hornet sends an advance patrol to detect a honeybee hive. Just a few hornets can destroy thirty thousand bees."

"I hope those things aren't still around!" Cami says.

I read on. The notes describe how smoking the bees from their tree and placing the crates nearby will make the transfer less invasive for the bee colony.

It says the bees in the oak tree are called *honeybees*. Then she writes: *The key is to make sure the queen is happy. If she shows hesitation, the worker bees will abandon her.*

"Let's get back to the hive!" Cami cries out. "Now that you figured out how to extract the honey."

"I mean," I say, hesitating. "That bee sting *really* hurt. And there are thousands of bees up there."

"Her notes are *really* detailed, Yoly," she reassures me. "And you know exactly how to read them. It took me *years* to even understand some of the terminology. It took you less than a day!"

"Well, technically," I correct, "I kind of understood it as soon as I read it."

"Humility does not appear to be one of your gifts, hermana," my sister teases.

I shrug and finally agree to go back to the woods to extract the honey.

Cami grabs her duffel and puts all the equipment inside. It hovers aboveground and she unlatches the drawstring, commanding it out of the shed. It glides effortlessly behind her as she walks back outside.

"Do you think that smoker will work on the bees?" I

ask, following behind. "I don't want to hurt them."

"Only one way to find out," Cami says, turning around. The duffel slides to a stop, and the rucksack carrying the giant smoker swings around onto Cami's shoulders. We head back into the woods to figure out how to get the honey from the oak tree.

Once we get to the branch bridge, we hike up and then drop down to the circle of small, yellow-flowered trees protecting the hive. Cami's hand grazes one of the wires that wraps around the enclosure.

"Did you notice that the copper wiring here looks just like the wiring all over the ceiling of Abuela's shed? She had to have been the one to put it up," Cami says. "Why would she go through all the trouble?"

It's a good question. One that I have been thinking about myself.

"I know from what Arelis has told me that certain types of copper wire jam connectivity. The Outer Valley was home to a large copper mine early last century. She thinks it's what's causing all their trouble connecting to the System." As I say it out loud, it starts to make more and more sense. "That's why there's so much copper wiring back at the shed and in these bushes! She wanted to keep the hive offline!"

"You sound like a detective from those cheesy Hortensia Blackburn mystery novels, hermana," my sister jokes.

"All this weight off your shoulders and you suddenly have jokes?" I crack back.

"Feels good to mess with my little sister and not have to get all motherly every five minutes."

"That's a relief for sure. 'Cause 'Cami-es-Mamá' is a pain in the—"

"Hey, I'm still your guardian; watch the language. *And* the eye roll!"

Honestly, sometimes I don't even realize I'm rolling my eyes to exaggerate what my sister is telling me. It's like a Cami deterrent whenever she's annoying.

The trees surround us, but I start to notice their distinct patterns. When I first came in here it all looked the same. But now I realize these trees are all unique pieces of a vast forest our abuelita settled near and sheltered her beehive in.

"Abuelita says we should get the smoker started first. It's easier to get everything set up before putting on the gear."

The gear is bulky and has a musty smell.

"We have to do a trap out?" Cami asks, trying to understand the directions that the book is telling us to follow.

I look at my sister prepping. She hands me a protective helmet covered in netting. At least Abuelita seemed to know my sister and I would work well together—even if she never actually met me. I smile at her face on the book cover's flap. It would have been amazing to know her.

"The drawing shows a cone-shaped device that is supposed to be attached to the part in the tree that has a hole in it." Cami shows me the book. "It looks like we have to use a smoker to get the bees moving out of the hive, but not too much or they'll get stressed out."

"Bees get stressed out? Go figure."

Cami lays some tools on the ground. There's something with a small lining and another thing with several comb shapes.

"That's called a nectar box," I tell her, finding the page in Abuelita's book. "We need a wire cone first."

Cami finds a wire and bends it into a cone shape.

"Now we have to place it on the tree," I say, reading. "We have to secure the wire cone to the tree to keep the bees from coming out."

The bees fly above us while we use adhesive to seal the wiring to the tree. Abuelita says the little hole at the end of the funnel is so the bees can come out but then won't come back in. Like we're removing them from their home and giving them a new one. We take one of the crates and place it right next to the funnel. We finish sealing the hole in the oak. The wire cone looks like we gave the tree a metal nose with hundreds of tiny mesh holes running the length of it.

"Abuelita says it can be anywhere from a couple of hours to a couple of days."

"We need the bees to get in that box so we can grab that honey up there," Cami says, sounding impatient. She presses a button on the fogger, and suddenly smoke begins to blast out rapidly from the nozzle.

I see her looking through the mesh hole, checking for bees. There aren't any bees floating around. She takes out the smoker and lights it up.

"What are you doing?"

She aims the smoker at the tree.

"Hurrying them up."

I rush over and grab the smoker out of her hand. She jerks it back. I pull again, but she pulls back harder.

"Cami! You're going to stress them out if you put too much smoke in there."

"This is what Abuelita wrote in the journal. This is how we can get the honey."

Smoke engulfs us. I cough and see the smoker has caught on the edge of the tree. The bees stay away from the smoke and start swarming us. I swat them off, but soon they're attacking my helmet. They're moving up and down my protective face covering.

Cami runs over and waves the smoker around me. The

bees disperse. Soon the entire area is covered in smoke. Bees are everywhere. We run as far away from the hive as we can. Around trees, up across the ledge, and right near the path where the dry creek leads us back to la finca.

"Cami," I say, trying to catch my breath. "What was that all about? We could have started a fire."

Cami powers down the smoker, and the fog begins to clear. Once we see the bees aren't around, we check to make sure the smoke isn't turning into a fire. There's a cloud still lingering around the trees all the way back to the hive.

"I'm sorry," she says between coughs. "If we don't get that honey, I don't know what else we can do. And I just . . . I can't lose you."

I rub my sister's back and try to comfort her.

"I'm worried we're running out of time. They'll take you away, Yoly. They don't care how smart you are or how good your grades are. They'll take you away."

I reach out my hand. She takes it, and I can see her breath calming. All my sister has ever had is worry. First about our parents and the farm, then her own survival, and then mine.

"We've got each other, hermana," I tell her, rubbing her shoulder. "We'll figure it out. Together, we are unstoppable."

Cami sets the smoker down and finishes catching her breath before we say goodbye to the bees and head back to la finca to regroup. Tomorrow we'll go back to the woods and wait for the bees to come to us. We can still get the honey. We just need to let them move into the box while one of us climbs the tree. But first, the fog needs to settle.

CHAPTER 12

The Comfort of Words

I spend all night reading and turning each page with care. Learning and spending time with Abuelita's words instead of scrolling constantly through the feeds and sites. I still like navigating through coding and programming to see what new application has been rebuilt from the old days, but holding paper in my hands feels, I don't know, more alive.

I still don't think trees should be destroyed to make paper, but books seem to have a magic to them when I hold them. Maybe because it's Abuelita's book. I don't know. It does make me want to read other books, too, though.

There's something comforting about reading and looking through her notes. The physical act of turning the pages is something I didn't even realize I would love so much. It's like having a secret only your eyes can see. The words move from the page to my eyes until I fall asleep to Abuelita's words making images in my dreams.

The next day, I log in to class and see Dr. Sime uploaded a verbal pop quiz telling me to name viruses found in nature. I think he's trying to throw me off, but luckily, because of Abuelita's book, I know about the *Varroa destructor*. It's a mite that can infect a hive.

"YOLA012108, you must use the Latin names and be specific."

"Well, Dr. Sime," I begin. "The *Varroa destructor* is a parasitic mite that attacks and feeds on the honeybees, or rather *Apis mellifera*. And the disease caused by the mites is called varroosis."

I can't tell if Dr. Sime is happy or annoyed, because his avatar has hardly any expression. He turns to his notes and scans a few files to see if my answer is correct.

"And how do you know about viruses that attack honeybees?"

"I'm studying more, Dr. Sime," I tell him. "Honeybees, humans, nightcats, you name it!"

"You will have an examination on viruses that attack the human brain," he says coolly. "I expect your capacity to study *bee* diseases will translate into knowledge of things that really matter. If it does not, you will be removed from the class permanently."

Dr. Sime carries on with class without giving a pop quiz to any of the other students. I swear he's dying to kick me out. And to think I couldn't wait to take this TIE class! It seems like all he cares about is making it as difficult as possible so I get booted out. Well, that's not going to happen.

Once I log out of class, I step out of the house and see the pollinator drones hovering around the field. I realize they look nothing like the bees by the oak tree. These are mechanical. Lifeless. I walk to the shed and find Cami reading Abuelita's journal. She figured out how to control the smoker.

"Can't concentrate the smoke in one place. And the fire has to be low and move slowly."

I nod.

"Ready for another try?"

Cami nods back and grabs our equipment. We head outside and toward the woods. The pollinators shift and move on the dried-out strawberry plants. I notice one of the drones stop in midflight and hover toward us. I stop and approach it. It hovers around like it's confused. I take the drone in midflight and hold it between my fingers. It's barely the size of my thumb, but not so small that a little camera can't be placed on it.

I put the drone in my pocket and open the pollinator

application on Cami's V-probe. The fleet shows up on the screen. They're all green. I reprogram the code and disable all functions. The drones in the field all collapse to the earth. Inside my pocket the drone lies powerless. I pinch it out and examine it for a moment before tossing it on the ground.

"Now not even these tiny little drones can listen to our conversations," I say, heading back to the woods.

"Nice," Cami says, impressed.

Cami and I move quickly past the trees toward the hive. Abuelita says it's called a colony. I like the sound of that better.

We arrive at the enclosed area and set about to execute our plan: We'll both climb the tree, and Cami will gently smoke the bees while I grab a honeycomb and squeeze the raw honey into a bottle I secured in my pocket. Then we'll keep the hive box attached to the tree to give the bees time to make their way into their new home.

Abuelita says sometimes two colonies will form if there is a young queen that can take on a new hive. If a queen bee is healthy, she can lay up to two thousand eggs a day! I can't believe I thought bees were death insects. *The Scourge* is not a very factual book, I've come to realize. It makes me wonder how many other creatures depicted in that story were nothing like they were in real life. Maybe Hortensia doesn't like animals, so she writes about how terrible they are. It would be nice if there were other books that showed a different perspective though. Like one about nightcats.

Up ahead, Cami's duffel still hovers aboveground. I notice a few bees buzzing around. Cami stops me before I move in.

"Let's put the gloves and helmet on," she says.

I fasten the helmet and put on the protective gloves. We decide not to wear the bulky suits again. They were too hard to move around in. The important thing is to protect our faces and hands.

We reach a few branches and start to climb. Cami moves around the other side while I approach the slit in the tree dripping with dark, amber-colored honey. I wait for Cami to start the smoker and let the bees evacuate.

The smoke starts curling around the tree. The bees come out of the hive and away from the cloud. I climb onto a sturdy branch and reach the slit. The bees are busy moving away from the smoke. I have a clear opening.

The comb is stiff and difficult to pull out. Honey drips onto my gloves and down my arm. I yank a little harder, and the comb finally gives. It's a beautifully dark square oozing with honey.

Cami reaches around the tree and watches. She gives me a thumbs-up and tells me to hurry. "The smoke is running out!"

I pull the bottle from my pocket and carefully balance

against the tree. The honeycomb feels like a sponge when I squeeze it. The honey drips into the bottle and along the side.

"I'm out of smoke!" Cami yells.

The air begins to clear out. In a few minutes, the bees will return to the hive. The last drops squeeze out of the comb. I place the last of the honeycomb on the branch and grab the cap to seal the bottle.

I make my way down the tree with the small bottle full of honey in my pocket.

"Nice job, hermana," Cami says, meeting me on the ground.

"Thanks," I say, handing her the little jar.

Cami takes off her glove and wipes the honey dripping down the side of the bottle with her finger, savoring the oozing liquid.

Her eyes light up.

"You have to try this."

I throw my glove on the ground and scoop up a little honey.

My senses immediately elevate. It's like no taste I've ever experienced.

"I can't believe Hortensia would write that bees were pests! Anything that produces something this good can't be evil!"

"Tell me about it."

I examine the hive box we left by the tree and see the bees starting to move inside. It's only slightly covered, but the bees aren't escaping from the top. I remember what Abuelita said about making the bees feel safe inside their new home. I put the lid over the crate and close it.

"And look at all of them, gathering around the wiring," Cami says, admiring the bees wrapping around the wire cone.

"They're starting to move in!"

"Yep," Cami says, putting the little jar of honey in her bag.

"Hortensia will definitely buy this," I tell her.

"And we'll buy back your scholarship," Cami says. "Get you out of that class."

"Yeah," I say, suddenly unsure if I want to completely withdraw from TIE. I worked so hard for so long. It feels like I'd just be throwing my future away. But I don't want to pay for my education by being forced into labor that could kill me. Even if it is "for the good of the community."

"First let's drop off our gear back at la finca; then we'll head into town. Go to the Exchange."

"Shouldn't we send a message to Mayor Blackburn?"

"No," Cami responds. "The Exchange gave you the scholarship. I'll tell Lucía we found a sponsor to pay it off and are requesting a grace period to finalize the transaction.

That'll buy us a little time while we find Hortensia and offer to sell the honey for agreeing to pay off the scholarship."

I look up to see the bees circling the tree. Ever since we ventured into these woods and found these bees, something has changed in my sister—in both of us. I'm happy we're here together. Happy that things are finally starting to look up for our family.

Cami packs up and starts back to la finca. I tell her I want to stay a bit.

"To make sure the bees are safely making their way into the hive box."

"Okay, hermana," my sister says. "See you back at home."

Just a short while ago, my sister would have demanded I come back with her. Telling me it wasn't safe. Now she trusts me to be careful. It feels nice to have a sister and not just a guardian telling me what to do all the time.

The space around the hive protects from any signals coming in or out. It's completely off-grid. Abuela wanted to keep the hive secret.

The bees hum quietly inside the box. They're happy. Yesterday their buzz was high-pitched, erratic, and frantic. Today it's calm, almost melodic. I open Abuelita's book and start reading while the hum of the bees travels through the air.

Bees produce broods, and those broods need to be in chambers so they can hatch and fly out to collect pollen. There's a place and a purpose for every bee in the colony. Abuelita says people were once like bees. People in communities had a purpose, a job, and they helped each other. They looked out for one another. Protected one another.

The bees continue their gentle buzzing. They crawl up and down the hive box. More bees enter the box, and soon several hundred have made their way in. They aren't bad like *The Scourge* showed. They're beautiful.

I look up where the hive is. It's hard to see, but when I was collecting the honey, I noticed a shine. I thought it was the sun peeking through, but it wasn't. It was more copper wire. Copper doesn't just block out signals; it's also a conductor for solar power. There is a tiny wire that runs the length of the oak tree. Almost indistinguishable from the bark.

"There's just enough sunlight to power this low-energy cooling system," I say out loud.

I close the book and start back to la finca.

When I get home, I drop off my things in the shed and walk to the porch. I sit and skim through more of Abuelita's book. She knew so much about science and flowers and bees. I tap her book with my finger.

There's an image of a plant. Or maybe it's a tree? The description reads:

Mahonia x media—mata con flores amarillas.

They're the same bright yellow flowers from the trees surrounding the hive. I read the description. They're not trees. They're some kind of bush. The bees use them. I keep reading through. Trying to figure out what Abuelita's descriptions are telling me.

It's like cracking code. Only instead of ones and zeroes, they're words strung together to say something. A scientific conversation of some kind.

I get a ping on my V-probe.

The System icon swirls on my screen. The happy little welcome penguin shows up randomly on my communication app.

Suspect Cornelius Rivera has been apprehended on charges of illegal connectivity and distribution of unauthorized literature. Thanks to our new AIF patrol, suspect is in custody awaiting sentencing. You are safe, Miss Yolanda Cicerón. Have a great day, and we'll see you in Silo soon!

I turn back to Abuelita's book, then look back at my screen. My whole body is a ball of nerves. Cami rushes out when she hears my V-probe crash to the ground.

"What happened?" she says, drawing close. She looks at me and then follows my gaze to my V-probe, halfway down the porch steps. My sister scoops it up and reads the note.

Cami throws the V-probe to the ground again, and the

look of worry turns to anger.

"They took him," she says, gritting her teeth.

She already knows what I'm going to say. The System found the FN. They're probably searching for whoever has a connection. I pick up the V-probe and look at the screen.

The FN icon isn't flashing anymore. Abuelita's book lies on the porch next to the V-probe. They took Cornelius for illegal connectivity and for having books. The System wants to control how we use information. They took Cornelius for trying to share it.

I usually blurt out what I'm thinking. It helps me organize everything I'm processing. But I decide to keep my thoughts to myself. I don't want the System to know what I'm thinking—or planning.

CHAPTER 13

In the Time Before

Cami and I are quiet inside the house and around la finca. We decide to go to Abuelita's shed to talk about everything.

"Cami, we have to figure out how to help Cornelius. *And* find Arelis."

"There's nothing we can do for them right now, Yoly," she says. "Let's stick to the plan. Get that scholarship erased and then figure out how we can help."

"You want to abandon our friends?"

"No!" she snaps back. "Cornelius is—" She pauses. I can tell how worried she is. "He means a lot to me, okay? And yes, I want to find a way to help, but until we get you out of debt, they have leverage over us. We need to take care of the scholarship first, okay?"

"I need to message Arelis on the FN. I have to know she's okay."

"Yoly, they just apprehended Cornelius. They might already be searching for us."

"It'll be fine," I tell her. "Arelis sent the FN to my V-probe on an encrypted file. It would take the System weeks to figure out where it was sent."

"How do you know?"

"Hermana, I'm good at this stuff, but Arelis is better. Trust me. She wouldn't send something that was easily detected. The problem is trying to find her before the System tracks down the power source she's operating from."

My sister looks at me like she wants to argue with me, but then her face changes.

"Okay, hermana," she says. "What do you want to do?"

I tell her tomorrow we need to head out at first light, and we agree to finish discussing in the morning.

"Better to keep our V-probes active so they don't suspect anything," I tell her, heading back into the house.

Cami says goodnight, and I go to my room. I lie in my bed, listening to the silence surrounding my walls. Walls that are surely waiting to record whatever sound I might make. But they won't hear a word from me. Not anymore.

I click on the FN icon on my V-probe. The screen goes

blank and the keyboard flashes. I scroll through our messages and land back on one of the first messages she sent. The letters I couldn't understand before scroll onto the screen.

SY<>FN. Panda. Bro. SI.ToC. Plsassist

I think *SY* stands for System. *FN* is also capitalized, so it must be Free Network. I look up from my screen. That's how she must be operating the Free Network. She's piggybacking on the System's programming! I look back at the message. The next letters are familiar. We used to abbreviate Silo back in the early days before the System upgrades allowed for more characters in messages.

I look up.

Cornelius is being kept in Silo. She must want me to find out where he's being detained.

I look at the V-probe. There's no way I can hack into the System. The fire walls are too secure. I could if I found the System servers and was able to access them. Every bit of data is stored in there. But I need a map. One that tells me where the servers are kept. I think about the old silos scattered around the countryside and their origins within the System. I know one place we might find some answers.

The next day, Cami and I plan to go straight to the woods. I decide to try to log in to class to make it appear like everything is normal. The moment I try to log in, a message pops up saying:

ACCESS PENDING

TIE doesn't offer any other explanation. Something isn't right; I can feel it. I leave my V-probe, and Cami and I go back into the woods, where I explain my plan.

But first we stop by the hive. We walk for about twenty minutes. I call out to Chiquita a few times, but she doesn't come. Cami says she's probably sleeping. Once we arrive at the colony, I see at least a thousand bees cover the entire wire funnel. I walk closer to the box.

"Cami, look!"

We gather near the hive box and see a large bee making its way to the funnel. It has dark yellow bands at the front of the thorax and middle of the abdomen. The tail is buff colored and is much larger than the others'.

"That must be the queen," I say quietly.

"Yeah," Cami says behind me.

As the queen makes her way into the hive box, I tell Cami about the copper wires that regulate the temperature surrounding the bushes.

"I was reading Abuelita's journal last night," Cami adds. "Bees don't fly out long distances when the temperature outside is too cold. They're usually more active in warmer temperatures."

"The cooler temperature in here must be keeping them

from flying too far," I deduce.

"Exactly," she says.

I open Abuelita's book and find the page I'm looking for.

"Those six-foot trees surrounding the hive aren't trees," I tell Cami, pointing. "You see the green leaves with the bright yellow racemes clustered around the bush?"

I put my hand across one of the mahonia leaves and show Cami the bright yellow flowers clustered around the leaves.

"The bees feed off the mahonia bushes year-round. That's how they've survived so long. They have an endless food source right outside the hive."

"So, the mahonia provides cover *and* food."

"¡Sí!"

"Amazing." Cami holds a leaf in her hand. "The bees must pollinate the bushes. They land on the flowers and take nectar from them to bring back to the colony, but they also carry pollen on their bodies that fertilize the flowers while they eat."

"That's why our drones are like that," I say. "They were programmed to copy the bees. To do what nature has done for thousands of years."

"Do you know what this means?" Cami says, coming close. "These bees can pollinate our strawberry fields."

"Yes!" I shout so loud a few birds perched high in the

trees fly off and scatter leaves in the sky.

"Wait," she says, pausing. "What if they only pollinate the mahonia flowers?"

"They're pollinators, Cami," I tell her. "It's what they do. They aren't choosy."

"The hive boxes aren't just for honey extraction," Cami tells me, looking through the journal. "They must be for transportation too!"

"Maybe Mamá y Papá were trying to move the bees. I saw them go into the woods at night when I was little. When you"—I stop for a moment, then continue—"when you were on Retreat. They would go into the woods, night after night. Cami, they must have been transferring bees to pollinate our fields! That's why we had that good harvest seven years ago."

Cami looks at the hive box, then looks to the ground.

"You okay?"

"Yeah," she says, collecting herself. "It must have been the bees when I was little too. But something bad happens every time, Yoly. The crops are good for a moment, and then they all die off. Don't you see the pattern?"

My thoughts go back to the previous day. Abuelita wanted to keep the System out of the woods. She didn't want anyone knowing about the colony or the honey, and this must be why. Time and time again, the past has shown the bees aren't safe outside the woods. This has to be the burden Mamá wrote about: protecting the bees. Everyone thinks they're pests because that's what's written about them.

"It's wrong," I say. "Hortensia's novels made people fear the bees when she values what they create."

"They aren't just for her honey," my sister concludes. "They're to help our fields grow. Not just ours though; all the farms in the Valley. But if someone fears them, they'll know not to go near them. Even if it's the very thing that might help them."

"If the bees were left to pollinate the fields across the Valley," I say, thinking aloud, "then Silo can't control what people do."

I realize that everything Silo does leads back to control. It was built after the people settled across the Valley. History class tells us that everything was in darkness before Silo brought the light back. They always seem to ignore that it didn't bring the light back *everywhere*. All the Westward System Expansion focuses on is connecting fiber-optic cables. What they really need is connecting points, like towers, to extend the power grid across the whole Valley. But there aren't any. Just sad empty towers around the countryside without connectivity. Like the old abandoned one on the Tanakas' farm.

"We wasted too much time here. We need to head to the Tanakas'," I tell Cami.

"Are you sure about this, hermana?" she asks. "It seems risky to be involving them. We could get them in trouble. And besides, we still need to sell the honey and get you out of that scholarship!"

I ignore my sister. She doesn't fully understand, even though I already explained my plan. My thoughts keep moving around my head faster than any fiber-optic cable can carry light signals as I work through my theory again.

The tower near the Tanakas' farm was built around the time the Valley was first settled, which means Mr. and Ms. Tanaka might know something about the early days of the System's expansion across the Valley and might have some idea about where the System servers are kept if the silo was meant to eventually be a connection point to them.

Every design begins with a blueprint; then data is collected and stored on servers. If I can understand how the System was created, like its original program code, I can figure out how things were built and where they're connected. It could be enough to wrench control away from the System and save not just Cornelius but the entire Valley. . . .

Because it's all connected.

"I'm sure about this, Cami! Trust me. This is important because it's not only the bees. It's the same with everything else," I tell my sister. "Connectivity. The System. The drones. Silo wants us to rely on them. The more centralized the power, the more control the System can have and the more—"

"Control Silo has," my sister says, finishing my thought.

The tree still has thousands of bees buzzing lazily around.

"Not for long, hermana. We're taking it back," I tell her. "Together."

Cami holds my hand.

"We're not just going to trade some honey to get ourselves out of some debt and walk away, Cami," I say. "We're going to figure out how to help *everyone* get free of the System's control over their lives. Juntas."

"Together," she repeats, and I can feel from the warmth of her voice that she means it.

"*And* we're going to find Cornelius. Mr. and Ms. Tanaka will give us some of the answers we need," I tell my sister.

"Even if they have what you're looking for," she says, a small pause in her breath, "can you really find him with just that?"

I know my sister has feelings for Cornelius. The way she talks about him is a combination of admiration and care. Maybe even love.

"You're worried about him, huh?"

She nods, then drops her gaze.

"We promised we'd see each other again one day. But we just . . . life is tough, Yoly. Cruel even."

I can see my sister's eyes get watery. I squeeze her hand.

"We'll find him, hermana," I reassure her. "I just need to figure out the original design map and get to the servers. Then I can code my way through to detect his signal."

I tell my sister that everything that has a connection to the System is built into an algorithm that communicates with everything else. Finding Cornelius is just a question of connecting the dots.

"Silo's power is centralized, so they definitely have to be keeping him somewhere in town," I tell her.

My sister seems reassured, but then her face changes again.

"No, Yoly," she starts. "This is too dangerous. My job is to protect you first, not—"

"Hermana," I tell her. "This isn't about me or you anymore. There's something bigger going on. It just took me a long time to realize it."

We unload our things and head through the woods toward the Tanaka farm.

Once we arrive at the edge of the woods, I see Ms. Tanaka inspecting her autocart. The broken-down tower casts a shadow over her house and onto a part of her cane field. She catches us emerging from the trees. I see her calling to Mr. Tanaka, and the two hop onto the rusted hover cart and move toward us.

"Camila and Yolanda!" Mr. Tanaka says, slowing down near us.

"Hello, Mr. Tanaka," Cami says.

Ms. Tanaka steps off the cart.

"Hello, girls," she says. "Is everything okay?"

"We're okay, Ms. Tanaka," I reassure her, eyeing the tower again. Ms. Tanaka follows my gaze.

"Are you sure *everything* is fine?"

"Actually, I have some questions, if you don't mind?"

"Of course," she says, looking a little concerned.

I point to her V-probe and motion for her to place it down somewhere out of earshot. She nods, and Mr. Tanaka takes both of their devices and moves the hover cart away from us.

"What's up?" Ms. Tanaka says as Mr. Tanaka places the V-probes far enough away that it can't track our conversation. He notices we don't have our V-probes.

"Tells us what's wrong, girls," Mr. Tanaka says, returning to us with a worried look.

"Our friend Cornelius was taken into custody yesterday," I tell him.

"I saw the alert," he says.

Ms. Tanaka shakes her head and sighs.

"We need your help to find him," I tell her.

"Girls," she whispers. "You shouldn't be getting involved in these things. It's very dangerous."

"The System has centralized all connectivity through Silo, Ms. Tanaka. The tower near your house was supposed to be an extension of the power Silo was producing, wasn't it? Why else would Silo have gone through all the trouble of building it? What happened?"

"There is nothing," Ms. Tanaka snaps. "It's an old tower from a long time ago. Leave the past in the past, and don't go looking for trouble. Okay? I'm sorry about your friend, but you have to keep your heads down or you will be next."

"Ms. Tanaka, please!" Cami blurts out. "We need your help."

"Did Silo share the original plans for the tower or the town when they asked to build it on your land? Did you save anything from when Silo was first being connected?"

"This is not a concern of yours and certainly not a concern of mine! You two girls need to go home and stop meddling, or you're going to find yourself in the same situation as your friend. Understand?"

Cami and I move back. Ms. Tanaka's scared. I can tell by the way her lips shake and she grips her hands into fists. I don't want to upset her, and she's clearly not talking to us. She moves toward her hover cart and climbs up. In the distance, Mr. Tanaka picks up their V-probes again and waits for Ms. Tanaka to come join him.

"Be careful, girls. You're playing with things much

larger than you realize."

"Abuelita was your best friend!" I cry out. "I guess you want to forget all the things you did together. All the sacrifices. You want to just bury those as well. Just like my mother made my sister do," I say, feeling angry they just want to forget the past because they're afraid.

"Come on, Yoly," Cami says, taking us back into the woods. I walk backward, still eyeing them. I can't believe they don't want to help us. "They're just scared."

Ms. Tanaka watches us leave. I can't tell what she's feeling, but I know Abuelita would be disappointed to know her best friend is turning her back on us.

"Vamos," Cami says, hopping back into the woods. I follow her in and start to formulate a new plan.

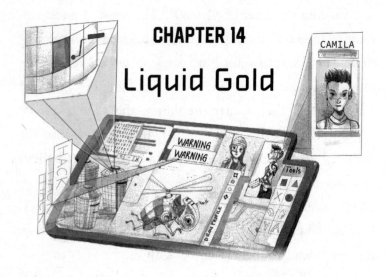

CHAPTER 14

Liquid Gold

We arrive at la finca and head into Abuelita's shed. We're safe from being overheard while we try to regroup.

"Well, the Tanakas aren't going to help," I say, pacing around.

"They're scared, Yoly," my sister says. "They've been through a lot."

"Doesn't mean they shouldn't help us. Somebody's life is at stake. And clearly whatever Mayor Blackburn is up to is not in the best interests of people living in the Valley."

"I know," she says, telling me that everyone in the Valley is quiet about it because they fear what will happen if they speak out.

"Fear is not a reason to stay quiet, Cami. And the people

all over the Valley need to stop suffering in silence. I see it, hermana. It's on their faces in the market. When we pass each other in the street or on the road. Everyone is struggling, and nobody is doing anything about it. We have to do something!"

My sister moves to Abuelita's desk and starts flipping through some papers.

"Hermana," she starts. "I know you've just started to realize how messed up things are around here. And I'm proud of you for wanting to do something—"

"Don't talk to me like I'm a child, Cami. I thought we were past that."

"Yoly," my sister snaps back. "I'm saying that the people in the Valley have been in this for a lot longer than you have. They have learned to survive, and we can't fault them for being afraid. Okay?"

I know my sister is right, but it still makes me mad. How can people ever expect to change their situation when they constantly live in fear of what will happen if they try? I want to get it done. I don't understand why other people won't do the same. As if reading my thoughts, my sister responds.

"You have incredible gifts, hermana. You're strong, and intelligent, and *stubborn*." My sister nods and doesn't let me interrupt. "It's true!" she continues. "Your stubbornness is not an insult, Yoly. It's why you've always done so well in school. Why you found the beehive and figured out how Abuelita designed the area around the oak tree to protect them. You even figured out the connection to how the bees pollinate plants and fruits and vegetables!"

Hold on a second.

"Cami," I say, interrupting her.

"I'm complimenting you, Yoly; don't interrupt."

"No, wait! Listen. I have an idea for how we can still get the information we need."

I smirk and ask my sister to wait while I step outside. The little pollinator drone is still deactivated and lying lifeless on the ground. I scoop it up and head back inside the shed.

"With this," I tell her, walking to Abuelita's desk and placing the little drone down. "All I need to do is reprogram it and run it through a private connection. We'll trade Hortensia the honey like you suggested. But run the transaction through Mayor Blackburn. Place this little guy somewhere on the mayor's clothes. And then we start tracking where he goes; eventually he should lead us to the System servers, and then—"

"Cornelius," Cami says, sounding hopeful.

"Exactly! After we plant the pollinator on Mayor Blackburn," I say, "we can meet up with Arelis at the farm."

"But wait; we don't have a private connection, Yoly. The System controls everything, remember?"

"We do, though," I say.

"The FN?"

"Yep," I say, as I open the drone up. "This is exactly why Arelis gave me access to the network she built. She knew I could use it to figure out how to help."

I continue telling Cami about my plan, and she agrees. We'll tell Hortensia that we figured out a way to make honey with the drones using technology and Abuelita's old notes. My sister agrees and starts making final preparations for our walk to Silo while I search for the little processor inside the drone's body. When I find it, I pull out the chip and start tinkering with the drone's connection.

We take the path through the woods, walking for about an hour before popping up on the south side of the woods toward the main road to Silo. I log back on to the V-probe to click on the FN icon one last time and send Arelis a note:

POLAR BEAR. MU@FINCA. NOCHE

All I can do is hope she sees it in time as we arrive in Silo.

I immediately notice there are tons of people from the Valley waiting at the Exchange. We approach the line, and Cami identifies Lucía, who is trying to answer questions. She looks uncomfortable, like she doesn't want to be there any more than the distressed-looking people want to be in line frantically asking questions.

"Let me go talk to her," Cami says, moving around the line toward her.

"Hurry," I say, looking for Mayor Blackburn.

Up ahead, just away from the line, I notice Ms. Tanaka holding her device. It looks like something really upset her.

"Oh, hello, Yolanda. How are you?" she says, acting like she didn't yell at us and tell us to scram just a few hours ago.

"Hello, Ms. Tanaka," I respond. Even though I'm disappointed she didn't want to help, I understand what Cami was saying. It's not her fault she's scared. I see her worried look.

"Everything okay?" I ask.

"Now that the flat pay is signed into law, the rates on property went up. The income increase means that the payments also increased. And the fine print says flat-pay credits cannot be used to pay off debt to the System."

You always have to read the fine print, I think.

Ms. Tanaka looks around for cameras or drones. We make eye contact, and I try my best to figure out what she's thinking. She smiles with her eyes but doesn't move her mouth.

She leans in and whispers. It's so soft I can barely make out what she says.

"Come over later," she says, then pulls away. She collects her things and walks across the street, through Silo's gates and back toward her house.

That was weird, I think. Maybe she *does* want to talk after all.

I notice Mr. McMillian leaving the line and grumbling something under his breath. His eyes are trained on the Town Welcome Sign. He looks up to nod at a few people from the Valley greeting him as he walks across the street.

He has a metal plate from his left shoulder all the way up his neck. Cami once said he had to get an augment to replace his thyroid. I think he got pretty sick. His wife passed on a few years ago.

"How are you, Mr. McMillian?"

"Not that good, Yolanda," Mr. McMillian says matter-of-factly. "Bank increased payments on my agri-trailer. And I refused the flat pay. I'm not giving up my land."

An AIF drone moves closer to us. Cami notices and leaves Lucía to come to my side.

"We all thought we were going to go back to our original ways. Using our hands. Working together. Sharing what we grew. All that tech and industry is what messed us up in the first place."

He looks up to the sky and squints his eyes. "I'm never paying anything back to these thieves!"

There's a flash and a low consistent beep coming from my V-probe. I look around and see other people's devices doing the same thing. Mr. McMillian doesn't have a V-probe with him. He looks around at the people watching him and then looking at their devices. I glance down.

Debt violation! Debt violation!

Mr. McMillian seems confused until he realizes what's happening. I back up, slightly afraid when I see those scary-looking AIF drones zipping through the streets toward me.

"It's those new Artificial Intelligence Force drones!" someone yells out.

The drones are sleek white silicone cylinders. They're each about eight feet tall with a base that hovers aboveground and move at incredibly fast speeds. Their extensions reach out to grab Mr. McMillian.

Cami stands in front of me and holds her position as the AIF advances.

"They're not coming for me, Cami," I tell her, moving to her side.

The AIF drones surround Mr. McMillian. Two of them lock into his wrists and ankles, and the other two hover in front and back of him.

Jacob McMillian of Lot 8839B has admitted to default. Subsequent fine requires maximum incarceration sentence until debt is paid.

Every V-probe pings. It's so loud it carries through Silo like a booming harmony of beeps.

The AIF drones lift him by his ankles and wrists and hover away with him down Main Street. Mr. McMillian raises his head to the sky and yells out at the top of his lungs, "You lie to us! The System lies to us!"

He gets zipped away and disappears into a building next to City Hall. I grab Cami's hand.

"What just happened?" I whisper.

"Sh," Cami says quietly, squeezing my hand. "Let's just get out of here."

"No," I say, pulling away. "We need to find Mayor Blackburn."

A voice calls from behind us.

"Well, that was terrible, wasn't it?"

Mayor Blackburn appears. "Mr. McMillian was a good man. A friend."

"Those things just dragged him off," I say, trying not to show my distrust in him.

"Awful," he says. "Unfortunately, those drones are programmed into the System mainframe. I couldn't disable them if I tried."

That's not true, I think. He commanded them to stop the other day when they surrounded Andrés.

"The alert said something about defaulting," Cami says, speaking more directly than I've ever heard her speak to the mayor. "Is that *another* new law?"

Mayor Blackburn eyes Cami like he's scanning her.

"It's more like a detention," he says. "A sentence given in the most extreme of cases. Well, exile is the most extreme of sentences, but we don't want to condemn someone to death, do we? Who could survive out there beyond the Dead City?" He puts his hand on my shoulder and gives it a gentle squeeze. "Don't let poor Mr. McMillian fool you. Jacob McMillian has refused to pay any of his financial obligations for years. I tried to warn him, but he's been stubborn as long as I've known him. I'm sure it will work out."

"But those drones said he will be detained until he pays off his debt."

Mayor Blackburn nods, then smiles cheerfully.

"That is correct, Miss Cicerón. Whenever he does that, he will be released without any further charges."

It feels like a convenient excuse to blame Mr. McMillian's detainment on his debts just when he decided to speak out against the System. Everyone in the Valley is in debt, but it's only Mr. McMillian who's being punished. No wonder people in the Valley are afraid to talk. Poor Mr. McMillian. He didn't do anything at all. I see Hortensia appearing behind the mayor.

She greets Mayor Blackburn without taking her eyes off me. My mouth goes dry. She's wearing a nightcat-skin pelt with matching pants. I almost fall when I see the night-cat's head dangling behind the woman's shoulders. My face goes numb. Chiquita.

She notices me watching.

"Statements of fashion are the sign that civilization is on the rise again, right, Herbert?"

Mayor Blackburn nods.

"One of our drones found this creature prowling the edges of the woods," she says. "It was vicious. Can you imagine if that beast had come to Silo? The carnage would have been horrifying! Luckily, we took care of it. *And* I got a new pelt out of it in the process! Win-win."

"She was not vicious!" I scream at the top of my lungs. "And neither was Mr. McMillian! How could you do this?" I move away from Mayor Blackburn. And watch as people stare.

Some people from Silo shake their heads like they're insulted at my outburst. Others from the Valley move away. Too scared to even breathe.

Hortensia stares without blinking. She smirks as people watch. Some in disgust. Most in fear. Cami is frozen, like she's unsure what to do or say. I know they can send drones to grab me at any moment. I don't care. They killed an innocent animal and grabbed a poor old man for being unable to pay his loan, or more likely just for saying what was on his mind. Stay focused, Yoly. Stick to the plan.

"Young lady," Hortensia says softly. "Such outbursts are unbecoming of an aspiring doctor."

Mayor Blackburn doesn't say anything. Nobody does. They all just let this horrible lady flaunt that poor nightcat around her neck.

"I wouldn't feel comfortable having a doctor who screams when she's upset performing such a delicate procedure as a neurolink operation," she adds through that awful fake smile of hers. "Perhaps it's her *upbringing*."

She glances over at Cami and then looks back at me.

"I don't care about being one of your doctors anymore," I say, clenching my teeth so hard I can hear them grinding inside my mouth.

"You were never going to be," she snaps. "Maybe all your research and planning failed to inform you that I am not only a renowned author, little miss, but I am also the designer of TIE and its most accomplished *professor*."

I suddenly realize. She was using an alias. She's Dr. Sime.

Hortensia smiles a devious grin, then whispers something into Mayor Blackburn's ear. The mayor looks back at me and offers a strange look. Like he's forcing himself to smile. She flaunts the pelt, then looks at me funny.

"You are expelled from my class and hereby barred from any future apprenticeship. Your debt is now due, and since you can't pay, well, I'm sure that your work on Retreat will be rewarding and incredibly fruitful for our community."

She moves to leave, and the pelt flops behind her like a flag with no wind. I chase after her and rip the scarf from her neck. She swings around and falls to the ground.

"You little creature! Herbert!" Hortensia stands and motions to Mayor Blackburn to summon the AIF drones. Two rush to her side with their arms stretched out toward me.

"We have something you want!" Cami yells, jumping in front of me.

"What are you doing?"

"The plan, remember?" she whispers, holding her hand out. I nod and straighten up.

"And what might that be?" Hortensia says, approaching. Everyone in town is watching closely. Hardly anyone has moved.

"We have," Cami starts, then corrects herself. "We *made* honey."

Hortensia's eyes widen into an awful stare.

"Liar!" she hisses.

"Our pollinator drones," Cami says, her voice shaking. "We made some modifications. They collect nectar now, and my sister built a processor to convert it into honey."

My sister recites our lie word for word like we planned. Mayor Blackburn knows we have access to Abuela's documents. It's not that far of a stretch.

"Prove it," Hortensia commands. "Where is this honey, then?"

Cami looks at me, then down at the pelt clenched in my hand.

"Yoly, give Ms. Blackburn her pelt back."

"No!"

Cami stares at me, and then I realize what she's saying. Mayor Blackburn is distracted. I nod and carefully reach into my pocket. I pinch the little drone and place it in my palm. I hand the pelt back and in the same motion reach for Mayor Blackburn. The little drone is attached to his back collar. He didn't notice. The plan worked!

Hortensia takes the pelt and swings it around her neck.

"You'll get your honey," Cami says. "Once we're assured my sister's debt is paid."

Mayor Blackburn steps in. "That's a deal," he says, looking at his sister and nodding like he's telling her something none of us can understand.

"We have to go home to get it," Cami says, lying again.

He just stares at me coolly. I can't tell what he's thinking, but one thing is for sure; Mayor Blackburn isn't smiling that fake smile of his anymore.

"I know you think you can hide away in those woods," he says. "But I will find you if you try to run. Have it ready, and we'll settle your debt obligation."

Cami is clenching her fists while my palms are a puddle

of sweat. Mayor Blackburn turns away as we start off. A few people from Silo sneer as we walk; some from the Valley just look down. I see Andrés. He's watching intently as Cami moves to the town entrance.

"Oh, ladies," Hortensia calls out. We turn around to see she's pulled the little drone off Mayor Blackburn. "I believe this belongs to you?"

She takes the drone in her palm and offers it to us.

My throat goes dry. I can feel Cami's breath shorten.

Hortensia drops the pollinator drone to the ground and steps on it.

"Whoops," she says, grinning. "Of course, you'll still have to pay the loans for the pollinators."

Hortensia stares at us. We don't say a word. Our plan failed. We totally gave up the only leverage we had.

"The mayor will be over shortly to collect the *honey*. I'm sure he's dying to see these *new* honey-making drones of yours too. Goodbye. I'm glad you had a *productive day in Silo!*" she says, mimicking the welcome penguin.

I hear my V-probe ping but don't bother to look at the annoying little welcome penguin avatar. I think of poor Mr. McMillian. Of Chiquita. I take my sister's hand as we walk back home. I squeeze it gently and she squeezes back. We're running out of ideas.

CHAPTER 15

Wash Away

Once we're far enough down the road, we turn toward the tree and go into the woods. We've become familiar with the area and know when to start looking for Abuelita's oak tree. After about thirty minutes, I spot the wiring up in the canopy of trees. We approach the hive and pause for a moment.

I'm glad we didn't bring them to la finca. Mayor Blackburn would have probably found and killed them. Cami examines the box. She carefully looks through the crate, making sure they're okay.

"Maybe we can live out here for a while," I say. "They won't find us."

"They'll confirm soon enough the drones didn't make

our honey, Yoly. They'll know we have bees *and* honey."

My sister says she recognizes the look. She says Mayor Blackburn twitches his eye like he's processing something and calculating what to do.

"He finds any leverage and exploits it," she says.

"I wish I'd realized that long ago," I tell her, hating the fact I ever trusted the mayor.

"I know, hermana. But we learn and move forward."

"What are we going to do?" I ask my sister. "I told Arelis to meet us at la finca. But Mayor Blackburn is going to be there. He'll take her!"

"Can you access the FN from here?"

"No," I say, looking up at the trees. "The copper wiring is blocking out the connection."

A mechanical buzzing sound trickles down from the oak tree. It's louder than any bee.

"What is that?" I say, looking up through the canopy of trees.

"It sounds like an ambush drone!" she cries out, trying to see through the twisting branches and leaves high above the ground.

"But the copper wires block the signal," I say, unsure now that the horribly loud buzzing seems like it's right above us.

"They can detect heat signals," Cami reassures. "Come over here!" Cami rushes over to the oak and climbs a branch. The bees fly around but don't swarm. They don't feel threatened. "The drones are camouflaged," she whispers as we hide, practically hugging the tree. "They have tiny cameras that reflect the environment around them. Makes them look invisible. On Retreat they were used to record areas where buildings had collapsed. Searching for anything alive. Then they reported back to base camp."

"Like giant wasps," I say, remembering Abuelita's book. We keep looking up to try to spot the drone.

The drone hovers away, and the distant hum carries into the forest.

"Let's go," she says, not looking back. "If they see us by the hive, it's all over."

We hurry up the pass through the twisted roots to the dried-out creek that leads back to la finca. Cami steps over some exposed root and pulls herself up to the trail using a tree to balance. I look up a few times, thinking I hear the drone buzzing above us again. When we get back to la finca, Cami uses the bions to scan the sky again.

"I don't think it followed us."

"I don't know," she says, then moves into the house. The door to the house closes, and I'm left alone outside still scanning the sky.

The buzzing overhead returns.

"It's back!" I yell but my sister doesn't answer.

I can't see the ambush drone, but I hear its distinct heavy motor. The designers could have given it a stealth engine, but they chose not to. Like they wanted you to hear the loud buzz from everywhere in the sky.

"Cami!" I call as Cami rushes out of the house.

The drone is drowning out every other noise, getting louder and louder. Almost like it's hovering directly above our strawberry fields. The leaves sway like there's a strong wind. The old pollinator drones blow off the flowers.

"Let's move to the shed!" Cami yells over the buzzing.

We run inside and shut the door. The buzzing quiets for a moment, then picks up again. I look out from the small window but can't see a thing. Suddenly the walls of the shed start vibrating. The drone is right outside. The buzzing shoots up to the sky, and everything goes silent again. After a moment, we open the door and step outside.

"It's gone."

Cami looks to the sky with her bions.

"It's the mayor!" she points, spotting a black SDV and four AIF drones speeding toward la finca. The ground starts to shake again. We hurry back inside. There's more rumbling. Cami takes off her jacket and stuffs her bions inside.

"What are you doing?"

"There's a back exit," she says, handing me the jacket. "It leads right to the woods."

"Wait, what? What are you talking about? We made a deal with him! We can still talk to him. Figure out another plan!"

"He doesn't care about the honey, hermana. He didn't buy our lie. He knew we would go into the woods back home. That's why he just let us go. He wants the bees and sent that ambush drone to track us."

"He knows where the oak tree is?"

"I don't think so," she says, fastening the jacket on me.

"We can't give up the bees, Cami; he'll destroy them!"

"I'm not going to give them up, hermana," she tells me, tucking the jar of honey and Abuelita's journal into one of the jacket's other pockets. "I'm going to buy you time."

"What? No, Cami," I plead.

"We can't outrun them," she says, referring to the AIF drones. "And you're the one who can bring this all down."

"No, Cami!"

"You're the last beekeeper, Yoly. Protect the colony. Find a way to save us all."

"You can't give yourself up!"

She presses a button. The jacket flickers; then miniature cameras light up across the jacket. It mirrors everything around the shed.

"They won't see you," she says, "but they'll be able to

track the camera signals. Make sure to turn it off once you're in the woods."

"Cami!"

She holds on to me, then puts her hands on my face. The rumbling continues. There's a loud beep vibrating the walls of the shed. It's the same sound the AIF drones made when Mr. McMillian was taken away.

My sister and I look so much alike. We could be twins. Her large eyes look deep into mine. She's been through so much. Sacrificed so much. I know she's going to do what she thinks is right.

An AIF drone sends an ear-popping screech inside the shed.

Camila Cicerón of Lot 2506, you have broken your agreement. Fine requires exile without ability for repayment. Prepare to be detained.

Yolanda Cicerón of Lot 2506, you have been removed from your educational privileges. Repayment of your debt obligation will begin immediately. Prepare to be detained.

Cami shoves me out the back of the shed.

"I'll buy you some time," she says, turning to see the drones forcing their way inside the shed.

Lights flash across the night sky. Sirens continue to blast across the fields.

"Apprehend," the AIF drone commands.

"Cami, no!"

"I love you, hermana," she says, slamming the back door shut.

I stumble and fall. The drones ransack Abuelita's shed. I crawl my way to the edge of the woods. I do as Cami says and turn off the invisibility mode on her jacket. I pick myself up and run as fast as I can to the edge of the woods. I see Cami being escorted outside. Mayor Blackburn steps out of the SDV.

"Mr. Mayor!" I hear her yelling in the loudest voice possible. "I thought we had a deal."

"No more deals," he snarls. "Where are they?"

"I don't know what you're talking about."

"The bees, *where are they*?"

"Bees are extinct, Mr. Mayor; didn't they teach you that in school?"

"Take her!"

The drones swarm her and lift her off the ground. Mayor Blackburn looks out into the woods. He's scanning for me.

"I know you're in there somewhere, Miss Cicerón," he calls. "There's nowhere else to go. Eventually, you'll come out and give us what we want."

He climbs back in his SDV and hovers away.

The lights from la finca grow more and more distant.

I run as fast as I can through the dark woods. I run and run to the only place I know they won't find me.

Through the woods down by the dried-out stream, I follow the path as quickly as I can. Finally, I reach the bees. I huddle close to the stones near the oak tree. My mind still racing. My heartbeats move faster than I can count.

"Cami," I say, fighting back the lump climbing up to my throat. I wrap my arms around myself and curl into a ball. The jacket smells like her. A mix of earth and grass. My sister is gone. They took her.

I can't push the tears back. They're already streaming down my face. I curl up next to the copper wires. The drones can't track me here. I take comfort in what Abuelita made. A safe place. Where my tears can be free to run down my face. And I can hold my sister's jacket until I fall asleep and wish this horrible dream away.

CHAPTER 16

The Last Polar Bear

My neck hurts from sleeping on the ground. I'm hungry, so I take a little of the honey from the container, and the sweetness wakes my senses. The bees are active, taking nectar from the mahonia bushes. There are tons of them. They do that to keep a good supply of honey and pollen when the temperature changes.

I check Cami's jacket and see that the System is offline on my V-probe. I click on the FN icon and notice a voice command has been added to the interface. Is Arelis updating the network from wherever she is? I press the new communication icon feature.

"Hello?" I call into the two-way. "Arelis?"

I hear only static. The copper wiring is blocking out

connectivity. I turn off the V-probe and decide to try to connect away from the wiring. It's too far to walk out of the woods, and there are probably drones looking everywhere for me. I haven't heard an ambush drone since the farm. I decide to take a chance. I'll climb a tree away from the wiring and see if I can connect.

I move far from the hive and find an opening where the wiring isn't wrapped around the top of a tree. As I climb, I remember that day when I first saw Chiquita. My heart sinks thinking about her.

I reach the farthest branch I can climb and pull out the V-probe again. I look at my device before turning it back on. I don't have much time before they can track me. I have very little connection, but it's something. The screen flashes, and I see the FN icon.

"Hello?" The sound crackles and a voice comes through. "Yoly? Are you there?"

"Hello?" I say, pushing the button to respond. "Arelis?"

"Yoly! You can hear me! It worked! You're on a virtual private communication line. The System won't track you."

"How do you know?"

"I hacked into your V-probe. I shut you out of the System. They know you're offline though and are probably looking everywhere for you."

"They definitely are," I tell her. "How are you? Are you okay?"

The static returns. I move the V-probe around to get better reception and almost slip off the branch.

"Whoa!"

I wrap my leg around the branch and clutch the V-probe. After regaining my balance, I try to connect again.

"Arelis! Where are you?"

The static returns. I can barely make out what she's saying.

"Yoly. I'm going to Silo to find him. . . ."

The message cuts out.

She'll never make it. They'll find her in seconds.

"Arelis, it's probably crawling with AIF drones! Don't go!"

She doesn't know everything that's going on. I have to warn her.

I climb down the tree and head north along the forest. I can reach the edge of town without being detected in the open.

After several miles, I finally reach the edge of the forest. The three large metal silos are shimmering in the distance. I almost see the Welcome Sign ahead. A door slides open along one of the corners of the wall. Just at the edge of the woods.

Mayor Blackburn steps outside. Three other people in bright-colored suits walk out with him. An AIF drone hovers nearby. It looks a little different from the others. This one scans around and seems to be responding to the conversation the mayor is having with three people who look like . . . AI? What are they?

The AIF drone hovers around like it's there for protection. It continues to scan the woods, probably looking for me. I duck to make sure it doesn't see me.

The robotic-looking people have metallic foreheads, shoulders, and hands. They almost look like those android helper bots from last century. But that can't be. Those things are completely incapable of operating. The tech was lost.

I take out the bions Cami tucked inside her jacket and look more closely.

"They're humans with robotic augmentation," I realize, saying the words out loud. "It's like they're cyborgs or something. They found the programming." I marvel at how they look like a blend of human and android.

I think about my neurolink class. Before I got kicked out, we were going over augmentation responses to neurolink implants. Full AI to human symbiosis. Dr. Sime—Hortensia—said it was to help people who were disabled from injury. I can't believe I admired Dr. Sime so much! They look like they were manufactured. Like they were put together in a factory and came out looking half human, half robot.

Mayor Blackburn hands a silver suitcase to one of them. He nods, and the three cyborg-looking humans nod back. They don't blink or smile.

A black SDV approaches. I look up and see it hovering next to them as they step inside. The SDV revs up and starts toward me. I duck farther into the bushes, hoping they didn't see me.

The SDV banks and turns onto the road. The blacked-out windows make it impossible to see anyone up close. Mayor Blackburn returns to the wall. A secret compartment opens, and the mayor types in a key code.

The door slides open. Mayor Blackburn looks out to the woods again. I'm still under the cover of the bushes so he can't see me. He checks his V-probe; then I see him scratching the back of his head. A small metal square shines against the sunlight.

Mayor Blackburn's neurolink is rectangular and has hundreds of connected fibers that seem to be running up and down his spine. It's much larger than any neurolink I've ever studied. What kind of device is that?

Mayor Blackburn says something like he's talking to himself, then steps back inside. The AIF drone hovers next to him as the door begins to slide closed. It scans back to the woods, but thankfully I'm well hidden. It blinks a few times, then zips inside behind Mayor Blackburn.

"Silo has a back door," I say, scanning to see if anyone is around. There's a rustle in the trees, and I duck my head in the shrubs.

A few birds flap away.

"Just some birds," I say, my heart racing. I put the bions back into the jacket's front pocket. "Why didn't you wait for me, Arelis?"

I continue to check Silo's perimeter.

I get a ping on my V-probe. The FN icon flashes like it's breathing. I enter the Free Network and see Arelis sent me a note.

Panda! I'm inside town. Need you to make a distraction.

The message icon turns off, and the communication one flashes. She's calling me.

"Hello?" I answer.

My V-probe speaker blares so loudly, I have to turn down the volume.

"Panda! Listen, there isn't a lot of time. I saw Cami on my scanner. I might know where they took Cornelius and her. But it's too guarded. I can't confirm for sure. I have a plan, but you need to get to town."

"Arelis, wait, we need to regroup—"

"What?" she says, interrupting. The line starts cutting out again.

"A plan," I tell her. "There's a back door—"

"Forget that," she says abruptly. "Walk through the gates. Ask to talk to Mayor Blackburn—"

"There's no way I make it out of there, Arelis. Meet me in the woods. Let's make a plan!"

"They're exiling them tomorrow morning, Yoly; we don't have time! Are you going to help me or not?"

I take a deep breath. I've been so worried about her. Now she's asking for my help, but it's going to put me at risk of getting apprehended. All she wants is her brother back. I want my sister back too. But this is bigger than our siblings. We need to break this whole thing apart. To end Silo's control over everything. If I'm caught, it will be all over. Cami's sacrifice will be useless.

"Yoly, please. They've been given a death sentence!"

I know how much pain she's in. I can't imagine life without my sister.

"Okay," I say, exhaling. "What do you need me to do?"

Arelis tells me to say I want a meeting with Mayor Blackburn.

"I can tell him I have the bees—"

"What? You have *bees*?"

"Not so loud, Arelis."

"Okay, wow, well we've got a lot of catching up to do."

"Tell me about it. Okay, what's next?"

"We need a key card," Arelis says after a moment. "It's

in his top pocket, but I can't get to it unless he's distracted. You talk to him about *bees* or whatever, and I'll do the rest."

"I don't know if this will work. He's got those drones!"

"I'll take care of the drones," she says. "I just need you to get close enough to distract him."

"Okay," I say, knowing she's alone out there and needs my help. "This is a *really* abrupt plan. I just feel like maybe we should think this through—"

"Yoly, please. This is the only way. They won't expect me. And I can momentarily disable the drones once we're out of Silo. We'll make a run for it."

"I hope you're right," I tell her, finally agreeing.

"I am," she says, then logs off.

Every other plan has failed. I might as well try Arelis's more cavalier approach to breaking our siblings out. Then maybe we can all regroup altogether. I guess it makes sense.

I walk out of the woods toward the first silo. It's dusty when I touch it. It always seemed so shiny and pristine. Except for the faded markings that always bother me. I wanted to forget. To keep the past out of my life. Only the tech from the past to rebuild the future mattered. That's what the System taught me.

I approach the marks. I've never been so close to them. They're so scratched out they hardly look like anything at all. But they're still there. A faded memory of the past.

I put my hand on the grooves. They're like scars that don't want to be forgotten. But there's no time for dwelling on memories. I regain my focus and march past the next two silos and toward the front gate.

I come up to the Town Welcome Sign, and the little penguin waves.

Greetings, Yolanda Cicerón of Lot 2506! What is your business here today in Silo?

YOLA012108: You know why I'm here, Penguin. Just ping him.

The little penguin looks on like it can't decide what to do with itself. Finally, the smile on its face changes to an angry grin.

Your meeting with Mayor Blackburn is confirmed.

I guess even cheery concierge penguins aren't in the mood for pleasantries anymore.

Proceed, Yolanda Cicerón.

As soon as I approach Main Street, Mayor Blackburn is already waiting.

"Well, hello," he says, waving me over.

He swipes the V-probe attached to his arm pad, and the AIF drone zips away. He starts communicating through his neurolink. He nods a few times, then turns his attention back to me.

"Yolanda, your sister went back on our deal. And after everything I did to help. I really thought we had a fair arrangement. And *you* have saddened me as well. Sneaking off into those woods. You've become quite unsavory, young lady."

"I'm here, Mr. Mayor," I say, trying not to show what a hypocrite I think he is. "I'm fine."

"Good," he says, raising his eyebrow. "I'm glad to see you're okay. Those woods are dangerous."

I see an opening.

"Mr. Mayor, I have the honey you want."

He seems to be communicating through his neurolink again. Suddenly, Hortensia appears, coming from the Exchange.

"Well, the honey *she* wants." I point to Hortensia, who is casually sauntering over.

"No matter how frantic a fly gets," she starts, "it will never escape the beacon that calls it to its shine. And once it touches it, *zap*! It burns to a crisp."

I force my best smile.

Hortensia presses closer. Her face looks like porcelain. Like she's wearing a mask. I've never seen her this close before. Her teeth have no blemishes. There isn't one hair on her face. She has two symmetrical lines painted above her eyes where her eyebrows should be. She looks both beautiful and terrifying at the same time.

"Where is the honey?" she hisses.

There aren't many people from the Valley in town. They come to town only on market days, and when they get notified they're getting kicked out of their homes. Mostly it's people from Silo. I start to notice their faces. They seem more augmented. Less human and more AI. Why hadn't I noticed how unnatural they looked before?

I pull the bottle out of my pocket and show her. Her lips curl into an awful grin. She runs her tongue across her upper lip. I notice a couple wearing the same clothes and sporting matching head augments across the sides of their skulls turn and stare at the little bottle. Hortensia is fixated on the honey. I turn back to Mayor Blackburn. If he's excited, he doesn't show it.

I really hope you know what you're doing, Arelis.

Hortensia reaches for the honey. Mayor Blackburn closes in. My heart is pounding so loud I fear everyone in Silo can hear it thumping. He leans in.

"Now give me the location of the bees," he whispers, and my skin crawls. "Or you'll find that your sister and friends are in for a rather *unsavory sentencing* tomorrow morning for their crimes against our community."

Just as Hortensia reaches to grab the bottle, a hand swoops in and snags the honey before Hortensia can grip it. I look up to see a girl with bright orange-and-green hair reaching into Mayor Blackburn's coat and pulling out a key card.

Arelis!

She shoves Mayor Blackburn, and he trips over the edge of the sidewalk and falls to the ground.

"I'll take that, thank you!" she says, clutching the bottle of honey.

Hortensia falls back. She shrieks and screams.

"Get that Outer Valley scum!"

"Arelis!"

"I got what we need!" she cries out. "Let's get out of here!"

She takes my hand, and we run toward the Welcome Sign. Arelis lifts her forearm and swipes onto the V-probe attached to her arm. The gates open as the AIF drones draw near. I can hear their metallic arms extending. One of their arms snaps at my ears. I duck out of the way as we cross under the Welcome Sign.

Arelis swipes on her arm pad, and the drone's arm drops onto my shoulder, and then the drone stumbles. I look back and see the white cylinder collapse to the ground. Two more race out after us.

"To the woods!" I yell, now taking the lead.

Arelis follows. The AIF drones are too fast. They'll be on us in moments. Arelis types on her V-probe as we run as fast as we can.

"Grab my hand!" she yells.

"What?"

"My hand. On three, grab it. One. Two—"

She doesn't wait until three. She throws me sideways, and the momentum sends me crashing to the dirt road just outside the woods. I roll on the ground and scrape my arms and legs against the gravel. I manage to look up just as the AIF drones descend on Arelis. Metallic arms extending. If they catch her, they'll easily take her down. I try to get up to offer whatever help I can, but before I do, she slides to the ground just as the drones are about to grab her. The momentum from their pursuit sends them flying ahead of her. By the time they turn around, she's already typing into the V-probe on her forearm.

Another AIF drone pops out of the secret entrance and heads toward us. It's the same one that was with Mayor Blackburn earlier. I pick myself up and run as fast as I can into the woods. Arelis isn't far behind. Once we reach the trees, we head farther and farther inside.

"What's the plan now?" I ask, trying to catch my breath.

"Keep running," she says, jumping over roots and through the bushes.

A few thorns catch my side, but I'm running too fast to feel the pain. The AIF drone is close behind. Its wailing siren rings incessantly in my eardrums.

"Wait!" I say, trying to figure out where we are.

"No time for waiting," she says, looking at her V-probe. "I hardly have signal here. And my disabling feature only works sometimes."

"Sometimes?" I yell. "What if it hadn't worked when they chased us out of Silo?"

"It *did* work!"

"Luckily!"

"Can we argue about probability later, amiga? We have to get away from that thing!"

"Follow me!" I say, taking the lead.

The drone is moving around the trees but doesn't seem to have spotted us. Arelis follows me as I jump over branches and down ledges.

"Where to?" Arelis says, keeping pace.

"Where the AIF drone can't track us."

"What are you talking about? AIF drones can track us anywhere!"

"My abuelita designed it," I tell her. "It has copper wiring all around it. There's no way to track or send a signal."

"Impressive!"

We keep running for about two miles until I spot the dried-out creek.

"This way!" I tell her, banking around the branch that's turned into a bridge. The drone's siren grows distant. It's looking for us in the woods, but the trees are too dense. And there's no navigation it can access. Soon, it'll run out of charge. And it won't be able to get back.

"Up ahead," I say, leading Arelis to the oak tree.

We both stop and catch our breath. After several moments, Arelis looks around.

"Whoa. I've never seen flowers so yellow before."

"It's a mahonia bush," I tell her, crossing through. "We'll be safe in here."

She sees the oak. Then the bees.

"Are those . . . ?"

"Bees. Yeah."

She steps back like she's afraid. I look at her for a while before it really hits me.

"I can't believe you're here," I tell her.

She's still watching the bees carefully. A baton dangles from a holster on her side. I see the scars running along her wrists and up her elbow. She doesn't notice me watching. It feels so strange seeing my friend, my only friend in the world, right in front of me. She turns around and makes eye contact.

"What's up, Panda? You look like you've seen a ghost."

"I thought . . . I thought something had happened to you."

Arelis is quiet. She looks back at the bees.

"Are they poisonous?"

I shake my head. She cautiously moves toward one of the stones surrounding the mahonia bushes and sits down. Her clothes are tattered.

"It's cold in here," she says, and I explain how Abuelita designed it for the bees.

She seems impressed. She picks up a stick and plays with it. She sees me noticing the baton. She swings her bag from her shoulder and plops it onto the floor. I feel the sleeve of my jacket, of Cami's jacket. Arelis notices.

Arelis pulls the baton out from the holster and throws it on the ground. "I found this up in the hills near a massive concrete roadway leading to the city."

"You went all the way out there?" I say, amazed she could venture so far beyond the Outer Valley.

"It's freezing. No power. No heat. I was able to squeeze some battery out of an old SDV tipped over on one of the roads. But it didn't last very long. Luckily, I found this," she says, clicking the baton a few times until an electric flame flickers on. She gathers a few dried leaves, twigs, and nearby stones to make a small fire. The bees don't seem bothered. I watch my friend warming her hand by the flame, waiting for her to tell me everything.

CHAPTER 17

Connectivity Surge

Arelis touches the oak. She puts her hand on the bark and looks up. The bees are busy with the hive. She backs up when a bee hovers nearby. It follows her, and she swats at it.

"They don't like being swatted like that," I tell her.

Arelis looks at me strangely.

"The death insects have feelings?"

I explain they're not death insects at all. I tell her they are actually gentle, beautiful creatures.

She moves away from the bee and examines the device connected to her forearm.

"There really is no signal here," she says.

"What is that?"

She looks at the device and then unfastens it. I examine the screen. It's like a V-probe, only smaller and it doesn't have the graphics laid into the interface with the apps across the main screen. The only icon I see is the FN.

I try to get a better look at the device while she keeps inspecting the bees buzzing around the hive box. She crouches to look inside.

"Be careful," I say. "They're not evil, but they sting if you aggravate them."

She backs away, then looks at the tree.

"They're all in there too?"

"We transported them into this hive box, and the rest are all there."

"Is that liquid gold?" She points to the honeycomb dripping amber-colored honey down the side of the tree. "Panda, you know what this means? We can buy out everyone in Silo! We can take over. Run the whole town!" Arelis looks up, amazed, pointing and laughing. "They'll never put us in debt again."

"They'll never let us keep the honey or the bees. Mayor Blackburn wants complete control," I tell her. "He's going to kill them off, take the honey, and destroy the last bee colony."

Her bright-colored hair twists in knots around the sides of her face. She looks like she hasn't slept in weeks. I can't imagine what she must have been going through all that time alone beyond the Outer Valley. I nod, looking up at the oak tree and watching the bees humming in and out of the hive.

"Abuelita brought these bees to start life over. Not for honey, but to pollinate our fields. Bring life back to the earth. We have to find a way to get the message out to the Valley. That the bees can help us."

"Everything in the System flows in one direction, Yoly," Arelis says, calling me by my name for the first time ever. "And the end point is always Silo."

"I know," I tell her. "But we can change that."

"Our siblings are more important. We have to free them before it's too late."

"Our siblings were fighting for something bigger than themselves," I tell her. "We have to do the same."

"I'm not abandoning my brother," she says. "Not for anything."

"We're not going to abandon them, Arelis. But we might be able to figure out a way to knock the System offline *and* save our siblings."

"I'm listening," she says, playing with her baton.

"I don't have an answer yet, but—"

"That's exactly my point! We can't do both, and if it's between the Valley and my brother, my brother comes first to me."

"Look, we may not have a plan yet, but when I do, all

I'm asking is that you trust me like I trusted you. Okay?"

She shuffles around, then watches me carefully.

"Okay, amiga," she finally says. "What do you have in mind?"

My thoughts start to wander. There are back channels within the System. Maybe that's where we can start? Places to access for maintenance and things like that. I learned that in school with Arelis.

"You remember a few years ago," I ask her, "when we wanted to see the inner workings of a fiber-optic cable?"

"And we accidently hacked the System mapping software!"

She laughs so hard she snorts. "As soon as we realized we were in there, we both hurried back to class."

"Yeah! Luckily avatars don't sweat, because we would have totally been busted."

Arelis pauses and looks out to the mahonia bushes.

"Seems like forever ago," she says wistfully. "Now look at us. Clothes all tattered, hanging out in the woods, me with this glitchy online program, and you and these bees. Not the lead programmer and neurolink surgeon living on Remembrance Road we planned for our lives, huh?"

"Tell me about it," I say. Just a month ago I would have never imagined being out here. Your world can change so quickly. All it takes is a step in one direction, and your life alters forever.

"Everything changed for me the moment I walked into these woods," I tell her.

"For me it was when they took Cornelius," she says, picking at the ground with a stick. "Those ambush drones flew in, and moments later the AIF drone dragged him out." She shakes her head. "They powered those things with routers connected to the SDV. They could have powered the Outer Valley like that, but they didn't. They just left us all out there to starve in the dark for years. And for what? To keep us working for them in exchange for scraps of power."

I don't blame her for being angry. For hating everything about this world.

"I ran as fast as I could," she continues. "All I saw were the last lights of their metallic white heads taking my brother away. Luckily, I had this." She taps her forearm.

"When did you program the Free Network?" I ask.

"Cornelius had been collecting loose cables along the hill roads. Old power lines that had collapsed over the years. Breakers, power cords from abandoned homes, anything electric. He gave breakers, cords, transformers—all kinds of devices used to run machines—to folks living in and around the Valley. He would fix an old heater and link it up to the System grid, then connect it in someone's house who had lost connectivity. He made sure it didn't draw a lot of power, so the System wouldn't detect the usage. And of course, his books," she says, her voice cracking. "They punished him for wanting to help people."

I'm quiet while I let her take a moment before continuing.

"He taught me everything I know. How to link System power to our own devices without detection, how to retrofit old programming software, even how to light that fire." She takes a few more twigs and throws them on the low-lit flame. "I have to get him back, Yoly."

"We will," I reassure her. "Both of them."

Arelis nods and pulls out the key card she snatched from Mayor Blackburn.

"I know it gets into his office," she says. "But I have no idea how to find it. I tried hacking into the System to find a map, but the fire wall is too secure. Mayor Blackburn has to have some access to the System mainframe in his office."

She was willing to risk everything on just the idea that she could get her brother back. No matter what. I can see her looking at me with a sadness in her eyes.

"I know I put you at risk, Yoly," she says, looking at the bees hovering nearby. "I just . . . I didn't have anyone else to go to."

She stares at the key card. "Some plan," she says, throwing it to the ground.

Then I remember.

"The back entrance to Silo," I tell her. "I saw him go in one earlier."

I scoop the key card off the ground.

"That door has to lead to his office. Or at least somewhere we can use this key card."

"That's it! We break in through there, then we use the mayor's key card to get into his office, find our siblings, and bust them out. If he has access to the System servers, we'll hack into it using the same back channel we found in class, take control of the System, and give access to everyone all over the Valley."

I nod, then add, "We're going to need some allies. People who will help us without informing the System."

"Everyone is afraid, Yoly. The System controls everything, and Silo holds all the power in those towers."

"People will help," I tell her, thinking about the Tanakas and the Méndez family. And Andrés and everyone who knew my abuelita and my parents and us our whole lives. We've all struggled and survived and occasionally thrived, but no matter what the circumstances, we've always relied on each other.

That's what Mamá was trying to say in her letter. That's what Abuelita wanted us to learn about the bees. Not that they make honey or pollinate fruits and plants—they do that, but it's much more. It's about the colony. A colony survives together.

"They'll help," I say, feeling a surge of pride run through me as I think about all our friends all over the farms running through this place. My home isn't in Silo. It never has been. I am and always will be from the Valley.

"I don't know, amiga," she says, dusting off her clothes, getting me out of my epic realization. "When things are bad, people's true nature tends to come out. And it isn't usually very pretty."

I throw Cami's jacket on, collect the little jar of honey, and grab my V-probe.

"Ms. Tanaka wanted to talk to me," I tell her. "Let's go there first."

"Okay," she says, sheathing her baton on her side.

We pack our things and prepare to leave. A moment passes, and I catch myself staring at my friend—there's an unspoken understanding between us. It's something I can't really explain. I smile, and she shrugs like being here with me is the most natural thing in the whole world. I realize that's exactly what it is—it's just . . . a connection.

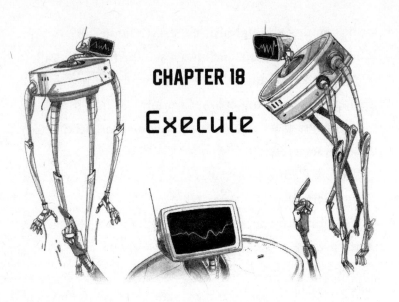

CHAPTER 18

Execute

We leave the mahonia bushes and the oak tree that's been a home to this colony for almost half a century. I put the container of honey in my jacket. Arelis and I take the path along the dried-out stream and head north into the woods.

After about a mile and a half of trekking, I spot the drone that was chasing us idling in a ditch. It's moving back and forth slowly, hovering, then dropping to the ground. I duck and Arelis follows. We hide in the shrubs until the drone runs low on power and doesn't move.

"I can rewire the drone," she says. "We can use it to block System access and go in undetected."

"An unexpected bonus." I smirk. "Are you sure this is going to work?"

"I mean, sort of?" she says, half smiling.

"That's not very encouraging," I tell her.

"I'll get it working," she says. "I just need to do it under five minutes, or—"

She pauses, looking around without finishing her thought.

"Or what?"

"Or it triggers its fail-safe and self-destructs. So, the way in is through the back. There's a plate—"

"Hold up." I stop her. "Did you say *self-destruct*? As in explode if you don't rewire it in under five minutes?"

"Give or take."

"We're going to need to reevaluate your risk averseness, amiga," I tell her.

"You have your procedural, scientific planning methods, and I have my fly-by-the-seat-of-my-pants-let's-see-what-works-and-what-gets-blown-up methods. Okay?"

I shake my head as she continues.

"These drones were originally designed as search-and-rescue drones. That's why they have those mechanical arms. But they had a fail-safe in case they were hacked and turned into weapons. It was the only way they could help and have some kind of defense against pirates stealing their hardware. Which happened *a lot* after the whole world started losing connectivity."

We both watch the idling drone as she continues.

"These things were supposed to help people trapped in places that collapsed when everything started going offline. Like smart buildings and cars and basically everything that was linked to some kind of tech."

"Wow," I say, amazed.

"People used to make tech to help each other. Until things got really desperate. You learn a lot about people when they're desperate. You know not everyone from the Outer Valley is nice. Some will do whatever it takes to make sure they survive and you don't. Like sell out someone you care about."

"Somebody gave your brother up?" I say, understanding.

"Yeah," she says. "They knew each other from Retreat. She was from our small camp. There are tons of little camps all over the Outer Valley. She got work in Silo, and everything changed. I didn't trust her, but Cornelius insisted she was on our side. She was trying to help. Cornelius told her what we were trying to do with the Free Network, and the next day we had drones around our home."

"I'm sorry," I tell her.

"I really hope you're right about your friends."

"I am, amiga. So," I say, looking at the drone again,

"how did you learn so much about these drones?"

Arelis shows me her arm pad again.

"I found one in the Dead City. It was completely stripped of parts but had a little chip hidden under its back plate. I dug up a loose fiber-optic cable, ran it through my arm pad, and linked the other end of the chip to see what it had inside."

"What was it?"

"A memory chip," she says, approaching the drone. "AIF doesn't stand for Artificial Intelligence Force. The letters mean Ambulatory Intercept Faction."

I walk up to her and examine the drone up close. It has a white sheen that seems to glow. The arms on each side are like weapons. They could tear anything apart. But they were never meant for force. They were meant to help. Someone rewrote their original purpose. How much more tech is being rewritten to serve Silo?

Arelis checks the network on her pad.

"There's still no signal, but I can bypass its hard drive," she says, looking at its chest plate.

Up ahead there are lights blinking around the woods. I spot two other drones looking for us.

"We have to hurry," I tell Arelis. She looks up and sees the drones about two hundred yards away. They haven't spotted us yet, but they are close and moving fast around the woods. Their lights are scanning everywhere.

Arelis places her arm pad near the drone's charge station. A light flashes.

"It still has juice. It's just in hibernation mode because of lack of connectivity."

I wait nervously, watching the other AIF drones scanning the woods for us. One AIF drone knocks over a tree branch, and I jump back. Any second they'll spot us.

"How long till it powers up?"

"Now," she says as the drone lights up. It rises and hovers above the ground, waiting. I can see the lights on its visor scanning. It's looking for a signal.

"With my arm pad synced up to its processor, I can change its coding," Arelis says.

"Hurry!"

"I'm going as fast as I can!"

Arelis moves her fingers on her arm pad quicker than I can track. She stops, turns briefly, and stares.

"You're breathing incredibly fast, and it's tickling my eardrum."

"I'm nervous!" I tell her. "Those things are less than fifty yards away!"

"Be nervous over there," she tells me, pointing to a hollowed-out tree.

I move away, and she continues to swipe and click on

her device. I tap the tree like I'm knocking on someone's door. Arelis stays focused. The AIF drones are circling. We're out of time. They're going to be on us any second.

"Got it!"

Streams of codes run up and down the drone's face screen; then it goes blank. Arelis looks at her pad, then at me.

"This thing is officially a helper drone again." She smiles proudly. "Under the control of the Free Network!"

I clap, and Arelis shows me the controls on her arm pad. I look around and see the other drones have left the perimeter. It's like they were called back or something.

"It will be able to access any codes needed to enter Silo. And help whenever something goes wrong. And knowing what we're about to do, something is *definitely* going to go wrong."

"Let's get to the Tanakas'," I say, moving ahead. The AIF drone hovers behind us. Following us through the woods. I keep looking back like it's going to grab us.

We keep walking north. There are a few openings in the sky, but I don't hear any drones hovering. Not yet anyway. The System won't be able to access our AIF drone anymore, but it will keep sending more drones.

We pick up the pace and rush through the woods, hopping over fallen trees and avoiding getting tripped up on branches. The AIF drone dutifully keeps pace no matter how fast we go. Even though Arelis has control of the drone, the thought of that thing dragging Cami off scares me. I wonder if this very drone was the one they sent to capture my sister.

We finally get to the edge of the Tanakas' farm. There's a clearing, and I see Mr. Tanaka tending to the sugarcane fields. They're still dark and sagging.

"Yolanda?" He looks worried. He sees the AIF drone and steps back. His cane-cutter bots stop chopping.

"It's okay, Mr. Tanaka," I reassure him. "The drone is with us."

I approach, but Mr. Tanaka doesn't move. He stares at the drone with a combination of fear and amazement.

"How did you do this?"

"My friend Arelis did it," I tell him. "She broke through its fire wall and reprogrammed its processor."

"And," she says while I watch her arm pad screen as she swipes, "I've disabled your V-probe's connection to the System and"—she finishes swiping—"given you access to *Free Network*. The FN. You're welcome."

Mr. Tanaka looks at his V-probe. "It can't be accessed by the System?" he whispers, inspecting it.

"No, sir," Arelis tells him. "It's with me now."

Mr. Tanaka smiles like he's relieved.

"I'm so glad you're safe, Yoly."

Ms. Tanaka rushes outside, looking terrified.

"Yui!" Mr. Tanaka calls. "It's okay. The drone is with them. This young lady reprogrammed it. Look!"

Ms. Tanaka steps away from the drone and watches as Arelis commands it to move its arms. She gives Ms. Tanaka access to the FN as well. If we could somehow give access to enough people, we could all start to communicate freely outside the System, I think. But it would take us too long to connect everyone by ourselves. And we're running out of time.

There's an awkward silence. Ms. Tanaka looks at me and offers her hands. I let her take mine. She gives them a gentle squeeze.

"I'm sorry I reacted that way the other day," she starts. "Mariela, your grandmother, was so brave. Always fighting for what was right. Like you."

"Arelis and I are going to Silo to take down the System. We're going to do it with or without your help, but if you had any information on the System's original design," I say, "it would better our chances. We want to free everyone from Silo's control."

Ms. Tanaka watches me carefully. She smiles a little.

"We have a map," she adds. "It's old though. Silo has

changed over the years."

"Can you transfer it to Arelis's device?"

"No," she says. "It's an actual blueprint. A design."

"Of what?" Arelis interrupts.

"Silo," Mr. Tanaka says, moving toward us.

"Ken was an architect," Ms. Tanaka says, referring to her husband. "He designed the blueprint for Silo *and* engineered the grid that powers the System."

"You did?"

Mr. Tanaka nods. "We built the central power grid with the goal of expanding," Mr. Tanaka says. "To give power to the rest of the Valley. It kept getting pushed to a later time. Making sure Silo was operational first. After years of empty promises, we decided to do something."

"Your grandmother fought to give us power," Ms. Tanaka adds with an air of pride and also sadness. "We almost got it." Ms. Tanaka looks at the broken-down tower near their house. "But Silo had grown too powerful. The System had already infiltrated so much of our lives."

I let all the information sink in. In all our years of knowing the Tanakas, they never once mentioned anything about this. The whole time they stayed quiet when we could have been fighting. As if reading my thoughts, Ms. Tanaka tells me they tried many times.

"Yolanda," she pleads. "Every time we fail, Mayor

Blackburn gets stronger."

"If you were part of all these *rebellions* against Silo," Arelis says through gritted teeth, "how come you weren't exiled when the rebellion failed?"

Arelis has a point.

Ms. Tanaka exhales, then tries her best to explain. "Mariela didn't pass away of natural causes. And your parents," she says, trying to measure her words. "Your parents and Augusto Méndez, Martin Sánchez, Andre Johnson, Shirley King, John Sarles, and countless others over two different attempts to bring freedom and power to the Valley—all suffered the same fate."

I can see Ms. Tanaka shaking. She looks tired. Worn down. I know that look. Cami has had it for years.

"Blackburn tried to make them talk. Made a public example of them. Used these horrible machines with pincers that attach to the neck like a metallic collar. He told them he would spare them exile if they gave the names of other conspirators. But they never did. Not one of them. And then those machines did their work."

Ms. Tanaka's tears run down her face. Mr. Tanaka comforts her.

"After that," she continues, "we all kept silent. We couldn't lose more of our people."

Her words settle in slowly. Like feet sinking into a

muddy pool. How could neither Cami nor I have known that Abuelita was exiled too? Was it yet another secret that Mamá y Papá kept to protect us?

My abuelita. My parents. All those good people. Gone for trying to give power to the people of the Valley. To distribute it fairly. I can feel my hands shaking. "Why didn't you tell me?"

"To protect you and your sister."

"Silence is not protection," I tell her. "It's just another form of control."

"Your abuelita said the same exact thing," Ms. Tanaka says, wiping the tears from her face.

"She was a smart lady," I tell her.

"So is her granddaughter."

Arelis steps in between us. "Do you . . . do you know if anyone named Rivera was also punished?"

My heart stops for my friend. She's never said if her parents were exiled, only that they were gone. I wonder now if she and I have yet another thing in common.

"No, I'm sorry. But there were many names. I might not be remembering them all," Ms. Tanaka says softly.

Arelis is quiet for a moment before she claps really loudly. "Well, I for one am super touched by all this beautiful rebellion, bring-power-back-to-the-people stuff, *but* we still need that blueprint in order to save our siblings before they get exiled too, so, yeah, can we get on with it, por favor?"

Arelis isn't big on emotion. She likes to get right to the point. I understand that about her. Sometimes you'd rather not sit with a feeling. Ms. Tanaka collects herself, and a determined look comes over her face.

"Third time's a charm, right, Ken?"

Mr. Tanaka nods and puts his hands by his sides.

"Come on," he says. "I'll get the blueprint."

"There we go!" Arelis says, moving to the house.

"Please take off your shoes," Ms. Tanaka says as she and Mr. Tanaka remove their old boots and leave them on a mat near the door. I press the unlace feature on my boots, and Arelis does the same. We leave them by the door, then follow Mr. and Ms. Tanaka inside the small house.

The drone stays outside, keeping watch for ambush drones or any AIF drones that may be patrolling.

Mr. Tanaka goes to dig out the blueprint from its hiding place; he returns with an actual map of Silo and lays it on the table.

"We may be old, but we can still put up a fight," she says. "And there are families who lost people who I know would stand and fight alongside you. María Méndez has lost many family members. So has Ms. Martínez."

I think of Ms. Méndez and her two small girls. I think

of Ms. Martínez and Andrés. They're all they have left of their family. Would they join us if we called? Ms. Tanaka looks at me.

"They'll fight. So would the Sánchez family. As we will," she says.

If we can reach the Méndez farm and then the Martínezes and Sánchezes and the rest of the people I know around the Valley through the System servers, we can give them access to the FN and they can spread the word out around the Valley. It could make all the difference. The Valley has more than five times the people of Silo.

But before I can suggest the idea, Arelis stands.

"I'm sorry, no offense, Ms. and Mr. Tanaka," she says. "But the Inner Valley has way more tech and connectivity than they did when Yoly's abuelita fought Silo. The people around here have gotten used to the light. What makes you think they won't be too afraid of losing it to risk helping? And besides, we need to rescue our siblings before we go off saving the whole world."

"Resistance doesn't die, young lady," Ms. Tanaka says, then looks over to me. "It just sleeps until someone wakes it again. Our farms are being taken, our children sent off to collect things in that frozen city, dying by the dozens. You sound the alarm, Yolanda." She turns to me and nods. "We will be ready."

A surge of pride runs through me. I know what Abuelita would do. What my parents would do. What Cami would want me to do. Rally everyone and get ready to fight.

"There's a long corridor here." Mr. Tanaka points to the blueprint. His finger then swings to the same back entrance I saw the mayor go inside earlier today. "It's only accessible through a password-protected door. You'll need to unlock the passcode."

"Passcode? All we have is this." I pull out the mayor's key card.

"They may have a manual lock for the inside. But you'll still need a passcode for the back entrance."

Our faces drop. We would need time to crack an advanced passcode, and time is the one thing we don't have.

"Put away those long faces, girls. When we said we designed Silo, we meant *all* of it, including the wiring." Mr. Tanaka smiles. "You'll be able to find your siblings *and* connect to everyone in the Valley."

"Like the mayor does with his weekly addresses?" I ask him.

"Precisely." Mr. Tanaka nods.

Ms. Tanaka then explains how to dismantle the security box for the passcode, detailing which specific wires to cut and the order to cut them in.

"You have to be careful," she warns. "It has access to every piece of tech in the Valley. It can easily detect you."

"I have that covered," I tell her, showing her Cami's jacket. "I'll activate invisibility mode and start searching for the System server. With that much tech running all at once, the jacket's video feed won't even make a blip if they're not looking for it. Once we find the server, we'll send a worm into its processor through the System's back channel and *boom*." I slap my hands on the table. "We get control."

"I'll be your cover and watch the back entrance to Silo from the woods," Arelis adds. "The AIF drone can go with you inside while I control it through the FN. You take the key card," she says, then leans in close. "Yoly, I know you want to save the Valley and all that, but don't forget—"

"I'm not going to forget our siblings, Arelis," I interrupt. "I'll find out where they're keeping them."

"Good," she says, then suddenly turns when the drone's siren starts blaring. Arelis looks at her V-probe. I glance over and see four red dots zipping across the cane fields.

"How did they find you?" Ms. Tanaka cries out.

"I thought the V-probes were disconnected from the System?"

"They are!" Arelis yells. "It's tracking from somewhere inside the house."

Mr. Tanaka starts searching around the house. I grab the mayor's key card from the table.

"We can't outrun them!" I say, thinking we're too far away to reach the woods. The drones will overrun us before we get to the trees.

Arelis pulls my arm. She grabs our boots and finds a back exit. "Over there!" she yells. We fasten our boots back on and run to the back door. Before we swing the door open, I see it. The little box in the corner of their living room blinking. The tiny cameras along the corners of the wall.

VOz.

"Mr. Tanaka!" I say, pulling my arm away. "The VOz box. That's how they found us."

Ms. Tanaka rushes over to the VOz box and smashes it with a club. VOz sizzles and reads out malfunction codes across the wall.

The siren blares again, and the drone calls out so loudly the whole house vibrates.

Yui Tanaka and Ken Tanaka of Lot 1392. You are hereby charged with abetting a fugitive, Arelis Rivera. Prepare to be detained.

Yolanda Cicerón. You are hereby charged with treason against the System. Prepare to be detained.

Ms. Tanaka takes my hand and ushers us out the door.

"Go, you two!" she shouts. "Finish what your abuelita started."

Ms. Tanaka rushes back inside and the door slides closed. I hear a rumbling of broken furniture. Mr. Tanaka yells as a window shatters and glass flies everywhere. Arelis and I duck out of sight as another AIF drone smashes through the door. I can hear its metallic arms destroying everything inside the house.

"We have to make a run for it!" Arelis yells, jumping out of our hiding spot.

"Wait!" I call out before she can bolt. "We can't leave them here."

"If we don't go, they'll take us too, Yoly," she says.

Arelis takes my hand, but I pull it away.

"Yoly, we have to go!"

The sound of drones inside the house fighting with the Tanakas thunders in my ears.

"Panda, let's go!" Arelis grabs my hand again. Just as I rise, I see two red lights flashing in our direction.

"The other two drones!" I yell as the menacing white cylinders advance on us.

Arelis quickly sends a signal to our drone. It responds and slams the two attacking drones against the house, immediately disabling one of them by running its arm across the back of its head—powering it down. A siren blares. Arelis and I cover our ears. Our drone wrestles the other one as Arelis and I hurry away.

"¡Vamos!" she cries out. I look back again at the Tanakas'

house and can't see anything inside—only a cloud of dust and smoke creeping out of the windows.

"Yoly," Arelis pleads, "we can't save them if we're caught."

She's right. I start to run.

The siren continues to blare as our drone keeps fighting with the other one. I look back and see one of the drones inside the Tanakas' house has gone outside and is advancing toward us. Arelis jumps in front of me just as it extends its arms to grab me. It pivots and takes Arelis by the legs. She swings her baton, but it falls to the ground. I rush to grab it. The drone pulls at Arelis while I charge the baton up. Electricity builds up around its point, and I strike the drone right through the chest. It falls, short-circuiting on the ground. Arelis gets up and we start off again.

A siren blares from the fallen drone like a distress call.

The fourth AIF drone rushes out of the Tanakas' house. Before we can get far, it swoops in and grabs Arelis by the legs. She flips upside down.

"Arelis!"

"Run! And take this," she says, dangling, and throws me her arm pad. "It has the FN access codes."

I fasten her device around my forearm as Arelis tries to free herself. The drone is too strong. It throws her down and grabs her by the arms. I have to go. If they catch me, it's all over.

"I'll find a way to save you!" I cry out, but Arelis doesn't respond. The drone has her completely pinned down.

I see the Tanakas' cart and run toward it. Maybe I can start it up and get to the woods faster. I hear the terrifying siren again and look back to see the AIF drone has broken free of our drone and is charging toward me. I'll never make it on time!

My lungs burn as I run faster than I ever have in my life. If it catches me, everything is lost. Cami, Cornelius, Arelis, the Valley, everything and everyone is lost. I can hear the humming behind me. The drone is gaining fast. The metallic arms extending as it draws near. I can't outrun this thing. There's no way I can get away.

Just as the metallic arms extend near my face, I hear a crash. I don't stop running but turn around long enough to see our drone has caught up to the other one and is pinning it to the ground, piercing its body with a metallic arm. The two drones wrestle and wrap their arms around each other. Finally, our drone rips the extensions off the other one and hovers above it making sure it doesn't get back up. I reach the cart and type a few commands to get the drone to follow me.

The sky is getting dark.

A siren blares again and I hear the familiar, terrifying hum echoing from the Tanakas' house. The drone that was shut down must have powered up again because it's charging right for me.

"Come on!" I say as the cart bangs forward. I look back and see the drone gaining. My drone is still holding the other one down. I have to think of something and fast.

I move the steering and start navigating. The drone closes in and reaches for me. I slide the control up, and the vehicle moves faster, dodging the drone but not before its arm grazes my jacket, ripping through the cloth and cutting my arm. It stings for a second before I regroup enough to swerve the cart, knocking the drone over, momentarily stunning it. I glide awkwardly side to side while I try to steer. It takes a few moves to get the vehicle steady, kicking up dirt as I try to gain control. It straightens at last and races along the road just as the drone regroups.

"Come on, cart, let's get going!"

The cart picks up speed and flies across the fields.

The siren blares again. The drone is getting ready to charge.

I keep going as fast as I can scanning the area and trying to think of a plan. It wouldn't be smart to head toward the woods. The cart can't navigate through the trees, and on foot that thing will catch me. I look down at the cart controls.

"I'll ram right into it," I say, starting to bank back

toward the incoming drone. The cart turns as the drone keeps coming straight at me. I push the lever up to go as fast as possible until it snaps and rolls off the center console. The cart flies toward the drone.

"Three. Two . . ."

Just as I make impact, I dive off the speeding cart and slam against the dirt road. My lungs get the air knocked out of them, and I roll around, scraping and scratching every part of my body and face. There's a loud *boom* as the cart and drone collide. I try to catch my breath but can't move. I open my eyes just enough to see my plan executed. There's one last siren blare that shoots across the Valley and my heart sinks seeing the faint red light emanating from the AIF drone that still has ahold of my best friend.

CHAPTER 19

System Override

I hobble back into the woods and wait for nightfall. My entire body aches from the fall. I should rest, but I have to keep going. Arelis's drone hovers next to me.

I can't believe I lost them!

My only friend in the world and the two people who were like grandparents to me. The AIF drone hovers idly by. I watch it for a moment as the pain from the scratches and losing everyone settles all around me. I can't do this alone. There are too many variables. Without Arelis or Cami or the Tanakas, what do I have? I collect my thoughts and try to focus.

They would want me to keep going. To keep fighting. I

made a promise to find Cornelius and Cami. Mr. and Ms. Tanaka stood next to me and said they would fight. After all those years of living in fear, they said they would stand by me. They said other people in the Valley would fight as well. If I don't try, everyone who has been captured or lost will have given their lives for nothing.

I pick myself up and dust off the dirt caked on my clothes. I'm not giving up. I owe it to my family. To my community. I have to think of a plan. The AIF drone moves along with me as I go deeper into the woods.

"I should give you a name," I say. The drone doesn't respond.

"How about Valle?"

The drone idles without so much as a beep.

"Since you're not objecting, then Valle it is. Come on."

Valle follows me through the forest. I can't wait until tomorrow morning to disable the System. It has to be tonight. Valle follows behind as we make our way in the cover of night toward Silo.

The walls of Silo are dark in the night sky. I check the perimeter for more drones. There were four at the Tanaka farm. Three were destroyed. The fourth kept ahold of Arelis. How many more drones do they have? I don't think they've brought more than ten online. Valle is repro-grammed. That leaves six to look out for. I don't see or hear any drones. The rest must all be searching for me across the Valley. The last place the System is going to check for me is right inside Silo.

Valle signals the secret-door entrance. It's about a hundred yards away.

"Ready?"

She hovers without response. I rush out from the bushes and sprint to the edge of the wall. Valle follows next to me. Once I get to the wall, I feel around for the secret compartment.

"Got it!"

I swipe it open, and a small screen lights up.

"Valle, get ready. This is delicate work."

Valle hovers next to the keypad and starts following my directions as I echo Ms. Tanaka's words to me. When Valle cuts the last wire, the secret door slides open.

Lights flicker on in the hallway once I step inside. Valle follows me in as the door slides closed. All I hear is the electric lights humming against metal—like a bee trapped in aluminum. The hallway is long. There doesn't seem to be a door anywhere nearby.

"We have to hurry," I tell Valle. "We're completely exposed here."

I run down the hallway and get to a corridor that leads to a door at the end.

"That must be it," I say, finding one of those early

twentieth-century doors with hinges and key locks. I take out the key card from my pocket and carefully unlock the door. It clicks open, and I press the jacket's invisibility mode on. The tiny cameras activate and mirror everything around me. When I step inside a giant room, the lights come on. Valle tries to follow me in, but I stop her.

"Stay here," I tell her. "In case someone comes."

She ignores my command and keeps coming inside.

"I said outside," I whisper loudly.

Valle scans the room. Her screen lights up, and I see the three servers next to a desk. The door shuts behind us.

Mayor Blackburn's office is larger than our whole living room and kitchen combined. There are monitors everywhere. His desk has a four-screen system that is hooked up to three different servers. Valle hovers over to it. She uses her arm to link into one of the servers—like she knew what I wanted to do. Her screen starts scrolling through the data and identifies it as a System server.

"It's all linked," I say, looking at how all the wires from the System servers connect to Mayor Blackburn's computers. Then I recognize a device from my neurolink class. It's a router that enables the neurolink to connect online. Like an invisible string. All these computers are running through that one neurolink router.

His neurolink is connected to *all* these computers,

which means he's hooked up to every device in the Valley. Mayor Blackburn is operating the entire System through his neurolink!

I can't reach people through here, not when he controls all the information directly. The System doesn't run independently. There's no use in trying to get into its back channel. Whatever changes I could make, the mayor could undo them with a single thought. But the opposite is also true. If he's no longer connected to the System, it all falls apart without his control. The only way I can dismantle its fire wall and free the System is by disabling Mayor Blackburn's neurolink.

There's a large coffee table and a sofa against the window with ceiling-to-floor blackout curtains. On one of the wall screens, I see live footage of Main Street.

On another screen, I see the interior of the Exchange. In the dark, it looks peaceful. Nothing like the scene that unfolds when the people working there tell someone they have to give up their home.

I look at another screen. This one is a little smaller than the others. It looks like it's a camera drone. It hovers across the Valley. I recognize the forest. It's la finca. The camera moves to a dirt street and up along a pathway where the trees are on one side and a patch of fields is on another.

The camera shifts up. Our house is in flames. My mouth

goes dry. The drone pans across the field, and then I see a fleet of drones swarming the field, the earth blanketed with smoke and ash.

Valle releases her arm from the server and hovers next to me.

"He burned it all down," I say, watching the shed collapse. There were over fifty years of life lived on that farm. He destroyed it all in just a few hours. My entire family history, left to ash and soot. I feel my anger rise. My hands clench into fists. He's going to pay for what he did. They all are.

I hear movement down the hall and quickly crouch under the desk and do my best not to breathe just as the door slides open.

The mayor walks in with two drones and a few people. I peek through an opening in the desk. One figure is very tall and has hair augments in three different colors and a metallic plate on his forehead and down his entire arm. Another has an entire torso made of metal. Her neurolink glows like an electric charge when she talks. Then my heart stops. Cami's friend Lucía is there. It was her. She was on Retreat with Cornelius and Cami. She turned them in.

Then I see Hortensia, still wearing the pelt. My blood boils. I want to charge at her, but I think better of it.

"She will make her way here tomorrow," Mayor

Blackburn tells the others.

"How do you know?" the one with the metallic torso asks.

He pauses and stares at Valle, then starts scanning the room. I crouch under the desk and wrap myself up into a tiny ball under all the cables. If he finds me, I'm as good as exiled.

"She was here," he says, still scanning, "but she scurried away like a scared little mouse. Probably tried to hack into the System with *this* thing but failed."

He examines Valle.

"We should go after her! She couldn't have gone far!"

"No," he says coolly. "She has nowhere left to go. We have everyone she's ever cared for under our thumb. She'll come, soon enough, to try to *save* them."

His head continues to scan the room, then Valle. Away from the crowds and the people, Mayor Blackburn looks almost robotic in his movement. It's terrifying.

"Silly girl. She's *inspired* by her grandmother," Hortensia sneers. "And like her grandmother, she will fail. Let's go." She gestures, and the rest of the group starts for the door.

Mayor Blackburn continues to scan the room. He turns to Valle.

"Herbert," Hortensia commands. "Have that thing disposed of, and let's make final preparations."

Mayor Blackburn nods and commands the drones. His drones rush Valle. There are two sparks before she falls to the ground.

He moves to his desk. His feet practically touch my head. If he moves one more inch, he'll find me. I hold my breath and try not to move.

"Herbert!" Hortensia hisses. "Let's *go*."

"We made a mistake leaving those woods uncleared."

"As soon as the fleet is ready," she says, "we'll knock it all down."

"We'll handle the bees," he says almost melodically.

"After you collect the hive's honey, yes."

"We can't have them *pollinating* like that old woman tried all those years ago," the large augmented man jumps in. "It will ruin our development plans."

"Yes! We can't have these people suddenly producing crops that can sustain them. They would pay off their loans! Silo would become insolvent!" the metallic-torso one cries out.

"All our work rebooting technological advancements after the destruction of the last age. The great plans we have for the reconstruction of the Dead City. It will all fail. We'll be in the darkness again!"

"Yes, yes, but before you tear everything down, remember, *I want that hive*," Hortensia snarls. "Lucía, did you uncover any additional intel?"

"No," she says, sounding scared. I can't believe she betrayed her friends.

"We brought you out of that awful hole in the Outer Valley, Lucía," Hortensia hisses. "We can easily send you back."

"Please," she begs. "I—I haven't had any luck with them. Cami hasn't spoken a word for days."

"*Cami?*" Hortensia says. "Is that a cute little nickname you call her?"

"No," Lucía says, but is interrupted by Hortensia again.

"When that girl comes into town tomorrow, you will have *one* more chance to prove your loyalty." Hortensia gets close to Lucía. So close I can see Lucía turn away and shut her eyes. "If you fail, you will be sent to the deadlands along with the rest of them. Understand?"

"Yes," she says, shaking.

"The ambush drones will make quick work of the colony in the forest," Mayor Blackburn says. "And we'll get your liquid gold."

I can see Hortensia's smile widen, and my anger rises to the point of exploding. I stay low and quiet, waiting for them to leave. My blood is like the honey that drips after being extracted. It's a slow, steady, thick pour of anger. The mayor escorts the people out of his office.

"Prepare the machines," he says to the drones. "Tomorrow we end this." He looks at Valle. "Send a cleaning bot to get rid of that thing."

The door opens, then slides closed. I wait a moment to make sure nobody is there. I step out from under the table. My invisibility mode is still on. I can see the screens on the wall reflecting on the jacket.

The drones tore off two of Valle's arms. The other two dangle at her side.

She's not moving.

"Come on, Valle," I say.

I don't want to leave her behind. They'll destroy her. Her face light flickers.

"Valle!"

She rises up and staggers a little. I guide her through the door and glide her down the corridor to the exit. Silo's back door slides open, but Valle pushes in front of me. She scans the area before moving aside to let me through. We step out into the dark of night.

The sky is cloudless, and the stars are out. The moon is directly above. I guide Valle quickly across the opening and toward the woods. We trek in the dark. He's taken everything from me. Now he wants to destroy the colony once and for all.

I get to the oak tree and glide Valle inside the circle. I check her diagnostics. She's hurt, but her internal processor seems to be okay. I take the wiring from the stones used to cool the area for the bees and hook Valle up.

The charge is slow, but at least it works. The bees won't mind if it gets a little warmer. While Valle recharges, I take out Abuelita's journal.

"What should I do, Abuelita?" I say, reading through her journal.

Abuelita knew everything about bees and their functions, especially the queens. The queen controls what the colony does. She communicates with all of them. I keep reading and thinking. The mayor controls everything through his neurolink. If I shut *him* down, all the drones will stop operating.

But how do I get close enough? I think about my neurolink class. The device is surgically implanted into someone's cerebral cortex. It's a delicate procedure. Once it's in, it's difficult to pull out.

"I can't just rip it off," I say, looking up at the oak tree.

It's dark, so I can't clearly see the hive. I use my V-probe light to try to find it. The bees are quiet. I can see a little dried honey on the bark of the tree.

Then it hits me.

"I may not be able to rip it off," I say. "But I can corrupt it. Get it to lose connection."

The copper wires are coiled around the mahonia bush.

"That's it," I say, closing Abuelita's journal. "But first, I need some backup."

Valle hovers quietly next to the rocks and stones. A bee floats by and lands on her shoulder. She doesn't move or respond.

I'm tired, but I don't let sleep take over. I think about Mamá's letter. *Find allies.*

I look down at the arm pad that Arelis gave me. It's easy enough to find the access codes she left behind as I scroll through the advanced interface. If the bees are my family's legacy, then this is hers and Cornelius's. And I'm not going to let their sacrifice be for nothing.

Mayor Blackburn has taken my family and friends from me, but he hasn't taken my community. He doesn't have enough drones to stop us all. "I gotta go, Valle," I say, heading back out of the hive. "I'm going to get some friends."

It takes me about an hour of trekking to get to the other side of the woods and down an open hillside to Ms. Méndez's farm. I knock, and she sees me outside her front porch.

"Yoly! What's going on?" she says, running outside. "I've seen AIF drones everywhere lately. It's like they're looking for something."

"Yeah," I say, "they've been looking for me."

"Are you okay?"

"I'm fine," I tell her as she examines me to see if I'm hurt. There are so many people in the Valley that care about our well-being. It's like being in one big family.

"And your sister?"

"They took her. And my friends. And the Tanakas."

She concentrates, furrowing her brow.

"They're taking away our homes, hurting our friends, restricting more access to the System," she says. "We barely have lights anymore. They just shut them off at random times. Say it's 'maintenance,' but I think they're just diverting power back to Silo."

"They're building a fleet of drones." I tell her what I heard in the mayor's office. "They'll be unstoppable if they have that many."

"You're here for a reason. Just like your mother y tu abuela." She looks at me seriously. "What do you need me to do?"

I take Arelis's arm pad and do my best to remember and copy what she did for the Tanakas. I find the signal for Ms. Méndez's V-probe and disable the connection to the System. Then I give her full access to the FN.

"The System can't track you now," I say. "And you'll be able to reach others across the community with the Free Network and give them access as well."

She inspects the FN and starts tinkering with the interface.

"This is incredible," she marvels. "Did you build this?"

"My friend Arelis did. They took her also. But she gave

me the access codes."

I explain how to find other people through the FN and show her the access codes so that she can share the network with others.

"Since it's using power that's piggybacking on the System, it's simple to reach people," I tell her. "But they'll know you're accessing their V-probes, so make sure it's people you trust."

"Okay," she says, understanding what to do.

"Tomorrow at sunrise, I'm going into town to save my sister and my friends. And I'm going to show Silo and the System that the Valley is ours. They can't have our homes. We have until then to get as many people to Silo as we can."

She doesn't tell me it's too dangerous. She doesn't try to convince me not to do it. To wait it out. Instead, she swipes on her V-probe and starts messaging.

"I'll ping allies in the Outer Valley. And I'll write letters and send the girls in either direction from our farm to deliver them to our neighbors. The Andersons and the Jacksons are good friends. They'll join us."

"Thank you," I tell her.

She comes close and puts her hand on my shoulder.

"Yoly," she says, the moon hitting the rough edges of her face. "We are and have always been ready to help when your family called. My father did. My aunt. And my late husband. We will always be here to answer the call."

My heart bursts with pride. I thank her and rush off to the Sánchez family. It's a forty-five-minute run in the other direction, but my determination to get to as many people as possible far outweighs my exhaustion.

I get to the Sánchez family and explain my plan. I give them all the access codes too. We huddle around their tiny house that's way too small for a family of six. They barely have enough seats for us all to sit. I notice they don't have a VOz.

"It mysteriously broke one day," Mr. Sánchez says when I ask about it. "It just *stopped* working."

He winks, and a smirk comes across his face.

"We kept telling them that we were waiting to raise money to fix it. But really, we just didn't care for those lousy books."

I laugh. The youngest Sánchez, Ivan, looks at the FN and starts sending messages.

Ms. Sánchez looks on admiringly.

"He's only six, but already knows more about coding than any of us."

I smile.

"He reminds me of myself at that age."

"We loved your abuelita," Abuelo Sánchez says. He waves his cane made of aluminum up to the sky.

"¡Estamos listos para pelear!"

I thank them and tell them I appreciate their help in joining the fight.

"Our community is our strength, mi'ja," Abuelo Sánchez says.

I nod, feeling a surge of pride run through my whole body.

My next stop is my last before heading back to the oak tree in the woods. It's Andrés's house. When I arrive, I see him outside. He sees me and waves, then uses his hands to tell me something.

"I'm sorry, Andrés," I tell him. "I don't speak that language."

He looks at my lips, then at my eyes. He gestures again and smiles.

"He says he can teach you if you like," his mother says from behind me.

I turn around and accept Ms. Martínez's embrace.

"That would be great," I tell her, then turn back to Andrés and smile.

"How are you, Yolanda? I heard about your sister. I'm so sorry."

"That's one of the reasons why I'm here," I tell her, then

look back at Andrés so he can see me speaking.

"The Valley is getting together to put an end to Silo's control over everything. I'm going there tomorrow morning, and then I'll give the signal using this." I show her my V-probe and the FN. She examines it, then hands it back.

She tells me she wants to help but worries if something happens to her, Andrés will be left alone.

"I'm sorry, Yolanda," she says. "I am with you and your family, but I can't risk leaving Andrés without his mother."

Andrés jumps in front of us and starts signing very enthusiastically. By the way he grinds his teeth and furrows his brow, I can see he's yelling at his mom.

"I know," his mother says while signing back. "But—" She continues signing, but he interrupts her.

His hands continue to gesture and move. His facial expressions go from angry to fearless almost in the same motion. Finally, his mother turns to me.

"My son makes a good argument," she says. She signs and speaks at the same time. "We'll be there."

"How do you say thank you in sign?" I say, looking at Andrés.

Andrés moves his hands and forms the words. I copy him and then hold my hand to my heart. He smiles and nods.

The sun is starting to curl through the eastern part of the Valley. It will be morning soon. I have to get back to the hive and make my final preparations. My legs are sore from running all over the Valley, but for the first time in my entire life, I feel like I'm truly doing what I was meant to be doing, saving my community like Abuelita tried to before me.

I get to the hive and make a spot next to the stones. Valle is nearly charged. I curl up with Abuelita's journal on one side and Valle hovering next to me on the other. I look out to the oak. The bees are mostly resting. I should rest too. Because in a couple of hours, I'm coming to Silo with my whole colony to end this once and for all.

CHAPTER 20

Eyes in the Dark

I leave Valle by the oak tree to protect the bees in case the ambush drone attacks before I can execute my plan.

"Remember to protect them until it's safe to come," I tell her, patting her shoulder.

Valle's screen is dark.

"Okay, good talk," I say. "I'm off. Thanks for all your help."

I walk through the mahonia bushes and take one last smell. I want to remember the sweet fragrance no matter what happens today.

The colony is just becoming active in the morning light.

"Valle will take care of you," I tell them. They

buzz around happily.

I reconnected the cooling system, and the temperature is already back to sixty degrees.

"Thank you, bees. You've changed my life. And thank you, Abuelita," I say, placing the journal in between the rocks and the stones.

"For the next beekeeper," I say, leaving the sanctuary of the trees.

It isn't long before I reach the entrance to Silo. I walk by the old markings. Still faded. I feel the grooves along the wall again. The markings will never be fully erased. Some things can't be hidden. No matter how flashy and technologically advanced a place tries to be.

I look up at the Welcome Sign. I used to love how the little welcome penguin would read my V-probe and announce my arrival. I used to think it was efficient to be so connected. To be online all the time. It was a way to bring us back from the darkness of a shattered world. But it wasn't that at all. It was just keeping us in a different kind of darkness.

The Welcome Sign outside the town gates flashes and sends a signal announcing my arrival. Four AIF drones approach. I walk past them and continue onto Main Street as they follow behind.

The citizens of Silo are all here. They sneer and hiss as

I walk by. There are only several hundred people living in Silo. Several hundred who control the fate of several thousand people living across the Valley.

I used to think it was the center of everything. The most connected place in the world. Nothing was greater. But it's not that big at all. One main road, a whole bunch of structures put together by the rubble of the past. A few engineers and programmers from a previous century, retrofitting and reprogramming things that were created and built long ago. But for their own gain and purpose. Silo is not a shining beacon at all. It's just a patchwork of scavenged pieces from the past.

Mayor Blackburn succeeded in bringing the Valley online and out of the darkness, but he failed at the most basic of all things—being a good human and sharing the world with other living things.

I see a platform. It's U-shaped and extends all the way down Main Street. The four AIF drones follow me down the street. The people in town continue to glare as I walk past them. I hear the words *traitor* and *disgrace* bandied about the crowd.

Mr. and Ms. Tanaka are on the platform. They're both tied down in chairs. A machine with two giant pincers hovers over them. The pincers twirl in constant motion over their heads. It looks like a hornet.

That must be what Ms. Tanaka talked about back at the farm. My heart sinks. There's no way anyone could ever escape from its hold. I can't believe anyone would create such a horrible thing.

I try to calm my nerves. Steady my breathing. Stay focused, Yoly.

Arelis rises from underneath the platform, tied and strapped to a chair. Unable to move.

Cornelius is brought up. His face is bruised and swollen.

Then Cami rises to the center. She looks hurt. She has dirt caked up and down her arms and face.

I feel my nails digging into my palms.

"Yolanda, so nice to see you," Mayor Blackburn calls out. He's behind Cami. He puts his arm around her shoulders. "Well, well, Miss Cicerón, it seems you've been a busy little *bee*, haven't you?"

I take slow, deliberate steps toward the mayor. Cami sees me. Her eyes go wide with fear. Everything will be okay, I try to tell her. Mayor Blackburn caresses the machine like it's a pet or something.

"This was originally designed as a medical device," he says, admiring the awful-looking machine. "Meant to sedate a patient while surgery was being performed."

He holds Cami's head. She tries to move it away, but her face is strapped.

"Of course, we've found a new, more practical purpose for it."

The mayor moves away from Cami and steps off the platform. The crowd splits and gives way to him.

"It wasn't long ago you were accepting our generous scholarship, attending school, a promising apprentice applicant, on track for a life as a neurolink surgeon, and now you're trying to *shut down* the System? Create chaos. Sow division."

He shakes his head.

"It's disappointing, Miss Cicerón."

I hear murmurs in the crowd. Like they're not happy with this new information. It's unsettling. People continue to look at me. They whisper. Their faces are a combination of anger and disgust.

"I would have made a fair deal," Mayor Blackburn says. "Even willing to forgive your TIE scholarship. But you chose to betray your community."

The mayor goes on about openness and fairness among the citizens of the Valley. "The dangers of selfish acts are bad for the community," he continues. "I've cared for you as if you were my own daughter."

His face changes. Softens, like the way he used to look when he walked around town smiling at everyone.

"I am willing to make one last offer," he says. "Give me

the location of the hive, or your sister and friends will suf-
fer the fate of exile, and you will live out your days alone.
Without your sister. Your friends. Or your bees."

He doesn't have enough machinery to tear down the
woods. There are too many trees. It would take him
months, years even. The fleet isn't close to being complete.
He's offering a deal because he wants the location of the
bees. He doesn't have the technology to quickly find them
on his own. I try to stall him.

"What guarantee do I have that you'll keep your word?"
I say, trying to make my voice sound brave. Even though
inside I'm shivering with nerves.

"Miss Cicerón, if I wanted to, I would have had those
drones detain you the second you arrived. Instead, I am
offering this trade."

"Yoly!" Cami tries to speak, but the awful machine
moves from Ms. Tanaka to Cami and clamps her neck.

"Get off of her!"

"Miss Cicerón," Mayor Blackburn says, walking toward
me. "*Yoly*," he mocks.

I stop. A gust of wind sweeps in kicking up dirt from
the road. There is a stale air in town. People have stopped
moving. I hardly even hear a breath.

"People!" Mayor Blackburn moves around, addressing
the crowd. "*This* is what happens when you go offline!
This is what happens when you lose *access*. The human

brain is not evolved enough to maintain control. *This* is what the System provides. It provides control! Look at this child. Look at her! She is untethered. Unconnected. She's put her friends in danger. Her sister. All of the Valley. And she has done this because she unplugged. She abandoned her trust in the System when all it ever did was look out for her. Care for her. *Love* her."

"The System didn't do that! It doesn't *love* anything. It's built to make us rely on it. To never be free from it. Or *you*."

I keep trying to make my voice sound confident. But it isn't working. I can see people nodding along with the mayor. Shaking their heads when I speak. I look at Arelis's device on my forearm. I have only a second. I swipe a message on the FN and hit Send.

"These people just want to go back to their lives, Miss Cicerón. To maintain comfort in what they trust. Not some twelve-year-old *beekeeper.*"

"Bees aren't bad," I say. "They're good. They pollinate our flowers. Our crops. He's lying!"

The mayor laughs.

"Have you ever *seen* a bee?" He gestures to the crowd. "They have giant stingers that attack when you get near them!"

I see people nodding. Agreeing. They don't know. They're so caught up in advancing their tech they've forgotten nature completely.

"Nature destroyed us once, but we humans know how to evolve. The next time Mother Nature tries, we'll be fully augmented and ready for whatever she throws at us."

"Nature is *not* evil," I tell him, hoping for some inkling of reason in his twisted thinking.

"I lost my parents. My brother. My entire family to nature's wrath," he snarls. "It's time I paid her back."

He starts to raise his voice. "And you, Yolanda Cicerón, have completely ignored your fellow humans and brought yourself to the mercy of nature's uncontrollable rage. You have committed the highest of crimes in our community. Putting nature above your fellow humans."

Mayor Blackburn looks funny. He's not moving his face, but his eyes twitch like he's scanning me. It's the same face he made in the office. Like it's almost robotic.

"What about *you*, Mr. Mayor?" I ask, my voice cracking while I scan the area.

"What about me?" he says, sounding even more robot-like.

Then I see her. Hortensia lurking in the shadows. Watching everything.

My fists clench in a ball of sweat.

"Well?" He scans my face like he's trying to read my mind.

I walk closer to him.

Extraction of a neurolink device can't be done without proper medical tools.

I don't have a laser.

Or anesthetic.

It's gonna hurt. I look at my arm pad. Where are they?

"Time's up," he says, moving even closer. *"Give me the location of the bees."*

I look at the dirt.

Mayor Blackburn lowers his head.

It comes out without much thought. Like a breath he wanted to release.

"And join your *parents* in exile."

I haven't had time to think about what Ms. Tanaka said. About my parents. And their exile. Even though I now know why they were punished, I haven't wanted to recall the memory of such a painful day. But blocking it out doesn't take the memory away. It just makes it angry. Scared. Vengeful.

I was there. Six years old. They raised us to the sky. Then the sun shone bright. I couldn't see Cami's face. I couldn't see the metal arms clasping my father and pulling my mother away. I couldn't see them being dragged off.

I ran to my parents that day. But they were loaded

into an SDV and sped away. I chased them all the way to Silo. Cami called behind me. Begging me to stop. But I didn't stop. I kept running until the shining towers came into view. The sun shone bright against the metal silos. I shielded my eyes as my parents were taken to be sentenced to exile in the deadlands. To a fate worse than death. A place no human has survived since the skies went dark and the earth came to the brink of destruction.

Cami stopped me before I could enter. She told me it would be okay. I scratched her. She peeled away and held her face. I took a rock from the ground and scratched the largest silo.

I dug into the glimmering metal.

I didn't write anything specific. But the scribbles were enough to show my feelings. Feelings that never really washed away. A memory I shouldn't have tried to forget. My family has been trying to take down the System forever. Every generation, fighting to take it all down and restore the world as it was meant to be. With nature. With power distributed freely and fairly across the Valley.

I look up from the ground. The mayor stands over me. His hands are raised high.

"Where are the bees?" he hisses.

I hear a ping. I glance down to my forearm. The FN

starts glowing. Like it's breathing and coming to life. Mayor Blackburn looks at my arm, then looks out to the gates. The Welcome Center gates start shaking. The cameras that scan people coming in and out of Silo start swaying. The doors to the entrance vibrate. The pings ring around the perimeter of Silo. The Welcome Sign keeps shaking and moving with the weight of people banging outside. The pings continue across the town. People in Silo look around, confused. Unsure what's happened. I turn back to the mayor.

"You see, the thing about bees," I say, looking over to Hortensia, then back to Mayor Blackburn.

I unseal the container of honey inside Cami's jacket and stick my hand inside. It sticks to my fingers. I can feel the copper threads pinching my skin—a mix of honey with Abuelita's copper wires. I turn back to Mayor Blackburn. "They don't like their colony messed with."

I smash the handful of honey and copper wire into his neurolink. The honey splatters everywhere. A spark of electricity fires out of the back of his head.

"Ah!" The mayor falls back.

"Valle, now!" I command into the V-probe.

Valle smashes through Silo's gates and races toward me. The entire Valley floods into town. People in Silo scream in panic, unsure what is happening. Everyone from as far out as the Outer Valley pours in screaming and yelling. Some are carrying sticks; others raising their hands in anger. More than a few are banging pots and pans and making a lot of noise. Valle swoops in.

"Change of plan, Valle," I say, pointing. "Get Hortensia Blackburn!"

Valle scans and finds her. She tries to escape into the Exchange, but Valle swoops in and takes her by the arm.

"What do you think you're doing? Get this thing off me!"

She tries to order the drones to attack, but they stand idle. Mayor Blackburn tries to wipe the honey off, but the copper wires keep jamming his signal. Suddenly, his head drops, and he goes idle.

"People of the Valley *and* Silo," I yell as Hortensia is moved to the center of Main Street. "Let's have a look at what Hortensia Blackburn has been up to, shall we?"

"Release me at once!"

"I would have never realized," I say, walking toward her. "Luckily, *Ms. Blackburn*, I know to look for the tiny details."

"Release me at once!"

I examine Mayor Blackburn. His neurolink runs all the way down his spine. She has complete control of his motor functions. He's like a puppet.

"You've been speaking through him the entire time."

"We are linked forever," she cries out. "It's what keeps him alive. With me! Get off me! He needs to get back online, or his heart will stop!"

"It's been you all along," I say. "Your brother has been under your control for years. *The entire System* has been controlled by *you*. It's why he never seems to age."

I can see tears streaming down her perfect porcelain face. A combination of rage and desperation.

"If he doesn't get back online, he will die. Please," she begs. "He needs my tether to stay connected. Please, I beg you. He's all I have."

"You devised this *System* twenty-five years ago. You put people into forced labor to collect scraps from the old machines to make this town that only serves you."

"I am re-creating the technological advancements and business advantages of the last great age! I brought us out of the darkness!" she says, looking at her brother.

"Yeah, but you also kept us in darkness," I tell her. "Valle, please free the System fire wall and let everyone have access to whatever applications, power grid, or information they want. And," I say, seeing the desperation in her face, "link Mayor Blackburn back up."

Valle releases Hortensia and moves to Mayor Blackburn's neurolink. Valle waits for my command before powering him back up.

I look back at Hortensia. She's desperate to get Mayor Blackburn breathing again.

"You're a brilliant scientist," I tell her. "Why did you feel the need to hide?"

"Nobody bothers you in the shadows when all they're focused on is the light."

"That's why the other rebellions failed. They never suspected you."

"That's right," she says, looking at Mayor Blackburn. A worried look returns to her face.

"Please get him back online," she pleads. "I beg you."

"You could have done so much good for the entire Valley. Not just Silo."

Hortensia nods, then sees Mayor Blackburn's head rise again. He starts breathing. Her look changes.

"Get them!"

The mayor kicks Valle and aims his arm pad at the back of her head. Valle shuts down and crashes to the ground.

"Silly little girl," Hortensia says, her face turning menacing.

Mayor Blackburn rips Valle's arm and frees himself.

He grabs my arm before I can react.

"Your grandmother took everything from me," Hortensia sneers.

"My grandmother was trying to rebuild a broken world!"

"That's what she told everyone," she says. "And my stupid older brother believed her. Then the storms came and nearly took him from me. When I fixed him, I vowed to never rely on nature again."

She moves close. This whole time it's only been about revenge.

"That's why you want to destroy the bees," I say, realizing.

She laughs uncontrollably.

"I don't want to destroy the bees!" She laughs. "I want to *take* them. Their liquid gold will be the new currency. No more credits at the Exchange. Just precious, delicious honey. And *I* will have full control of it."

"Wow, that's—that's not what I was expecting you to say."

She looks at me.

"I restored our society from a world controlled by nature. *You* want to take us back to scavenging for scraps of food. Fighting for shelter. Running from feral animals."

She pauses like she's lost in thought.

"I was just a little girl when everything was taken from me. For twenty-five years, I've been rebuilding and preparing to take it all back. Put Miss Cicerón in her place," she commands.

Mayor Blackburn drags me to the ground. My wrist twists and feels like it's about to break.

"The System keeps everything in control!" she sneers.

The pain shoots from my wrist to my shoulder. It feels like he's going to rip my hand off.

"You . . . you didn't protect us," I say, barely able to stand the pain. "You . . . you exploited us. Nature isn't the enemy. You are."

Mayor Blackburn raises his hand to the sky. I close my eyes, bracing for impact.

I open them wide enough to see a pair of boots kicking up dirt at lightning speed.

"Get your hands off mi hermana!"

Cami tackles Hortensia. Mayor Blackburn lets go of my wrist, and his head drops again. Hortensia wrestles around with Cami. She knocks my sister down. She's about to strike when Lucía sweeps in and pushes her to the ground.

"You traitor!" Hortensia yells, getting up.

"Not anymore," Lucía says, helping Cami up.

Arelis frees herself from the straps. The mayor stays idle. Arelis darts toward Hortensia and helps Cami and Lucía restrain her.

"I was protecting you all!" she cries out. "I was keeping you safe!"

Mr. and Ms. Tanaka free themselves. Lucía and Arelis hold Hortensia. Her hair unravels in her face. Her eyes are pools of red.

"You'll never survive without me. You'll be ruined. *All of you!*"

Hortensia cowers when Arelis reaches for her neurolink. "No, please!" she cries out.

"Stop!" I tell Arelis. "If you disable her neurolink"—I point to Mayor Blackburn—"he'll die. And we're not killers, amiga."

Arelis pulls back. She knows I'm right. I look over to Mayor Blackburn, all helpless and defeated. He can stay connected to his sister, but he'll never have all that power again. Neither of them will.

I can see people from the Valley filling the streets. They're chanting and declaring their freedom from the System's control. From Silo's grip on their lives. They're standing together like a unified group.

I see Andrés standing proud with his hands at his side, ready for anything.

Ms. Méndez is yelling "Freedom from Silo!" at the top of her lungs. Her daughters join her.

Abuelito Sánchez is waving his cane. He repeats, "¡Libertad! ¡Libertad!" over and over again.

There are so many allies. So many friends. They came. They all came. They're not hurting anyone or threatening to destroy anything. They're all just standing together. Like a colony ready to defend the hive.

I hobble over to my sister.

"You okay?" she asks, touching my wrist.

"I think it's broken," I say, clutching it.

Cami puts her arm around me. She hugs me, and the world melts away.

"I need a nap," I tell her, leaning my head on her shoulder.

We take a quiet moment together amid all the celebration.

"You figured it out," Cami says, smiling. "Can't say I'm surprised."

"I mean, there were, like, *ten* plans that didn't work, hermana," I tell her. "It wasn't exactly clean execution, you know?"

"But you never stopped trying," she says, pulling me in. I smile, feeling the warmth of her embrace. I pull back and watch Hortensia in the distance.

"You know," I tell Cami, "a part of me is kind of impressed with her?"

"I'm not sure subjugating an entire population to her will because she has some vendetta against nature and our abuelita is my idea of impressive but go on."

"She's brilliant," I admit. "She devised *everything* in Silo. Reprogrammed all those drones, the SDVs, figured out cyborg genetic programming, devised the entire System. And she started when she was my age. Not even Abuelita could stop her."

"You're just as brilliant as she is, hermana," Cami says,

pulling me close. "But you chose to use your intelligence to *help* your community. She used her abilities to control everything."

I nod. She's right. But a part of me still feels sad for Hortensia.

I realize I know why I'm feeling this way and tell Cami so. Hortensia has nobody. Just the shell of a brother who can't survive without her. We can make terrible mistakes when we feel desperate and alone.

"That's what makes you so special, hermana," she says, wrapping her arm around me.

"What?"

"Tu corazón," she says, pointing to my chest.

People in the Valley walk around Silo as the people from town look like they're going to get eaten by wild animals. This whole time they were more afraid of us than we were of them.

I find Hortensia, and she cowers like I'm going to hit her.

"I'm not going to hit you," I tell her, ripping Chiquita's pelt off her neck. She twists and nearly falls. She's taken away and placed in a holding cell along with Mayor Blackburn and those two augmented people from the mayor's office. They don't fight or argue as they're escorted away.

We leave the rest of Silo's citizens alone.

"They've committed no crime," I say, even though people in the Valley want justice for all the years Silo's citizens never helped, or even cared, about the struggles and hardships we all had to endure for so long. "There is blame in their silence and indifference. But Silo's citizens no longer work for the System. Any engineer, programmer, software developer, or medical personnel will have to start making house calls around the Valley."

Once we figure out how to stabilize Hortensia's and the mayor's neurolinks, we shut down the System at last. Arelis uploads the Free Network and gives access codes to everyone. I hug the Tanakas and thank them for everything. Ms. Tanaka cries and says how proud she is. They're the closest thing to grandparents we have in the Valley. I appreciate them more than I can ever say. After everyone returns to their homes, I turn to Cami, feeling like I haven't slept in weeks.

My sister and I, together with Cornelius and Arelis, start back to la finca to see what can be salvaged from the fire. The little welcome penguin greets us as we leave.

Yolanda Cicerón of Lot 2506, we hope you had a productive day in Silo!

"Sure did, Mr. Penguin. Sure did."

We go into the woods with a newly repowered Valle following us, not too far behind.

At some point, we stop and make a place to bury Chiquita and say our goodbyes. It still hurts to know she's gone.

"I wish I would have known her longer," I say.

"Me too, hermanita," Cami responds.

So much in nature is taken for granted. Yes, it can be scary and dangerous, but that doesn't mean we destroy it. Hortensia was so full of rage, she blinded herself.

I sit near the little mound for a moment. Chiquita was the first creature I met on this journey. She was the one to introduce me to the beauty and power of nature. My hand rests on the mound. I'm going to miss her.

We continue to hike through the woods, and Arelis walks with me.

She tells me to keep the arm device.

"Looks better on you anyway," she says, playfully shoving me while Cami inspects Valle and shakes her head.

"This thing only has one arm now, Yoly," she says, staring. "You sure you don't want to sync up with one of the other drones?"

"Nah, Valle's perfect," I tell her.

We step over the branches and down toward the dried-up creek. We pass by the oak to check on the bees. Cornelius marvels at how beautiful they are.

"I'm sorry," he tells Arelis while I admire the mahonias. "I should have never put you in danger, hermana."

"Danger? Yeah, right, as if a thing like danger ever

stopped me." Arelis punches her brother in the shoulder. "Glad you're okay, Stink Face," she teases.

"You too, Arelis."

Cami and I walk ahead, side by side, to give them some privacy as they catch up. Cami's mostly quiet.

"So," she says after a little while, "you know the hive actually listens to the queen. Not the *community*."

Cami winks and grins.

"I'm definitely *not* any kind of queen, Cami. Don't start."

"Oh, I was referring to myself," she corrects.

"What? Yeah, right!"

"I asked you to read Abuelita's book, and you went off into the woods and changed the world. So basically, you were listening to your queen."

"Yeah right! As if." I throw my shoulder into hers. "If anything, *I'm* the queen."

"I think I'm the queen."

"Get over yourself, hermana. I *saved you*, remember?"

"But I saved you first."

"Ladies!" Arelis interrupts, putting her arms around both of us. "You can *both* be queens, okay?"

Cami and I look at each other.

"There *are* two queens," I say.

"The hive box and the oak tree."

"I got the oak; you get the little itty-bitty box," Cami says, giving me a pat and rushing off before I can answer.

"Hey! Yeah, right! You get the little hive box!"

I hear Cami laughing and letting Cornelius catch up to us. She swings her arms around his broad shoulders and makes him carry her through the woods. I've never seen my sister so carefree. It's the best feeling in the world to watch her like that.

I hear a small whimper just outside the mahonia bushes. I move to inspect. Cami and Arelis follow. Inside a small hole in the ground, a nightcat cub shivers and whimpers. It's so skinny. It looks like it's starving. I put my hand out.

"Hey," I say, unafraid.

The little cub watches me, deciding if it wants to trust me or not.

"Cami," I whisper, "hand me a protein cube."

Cami pulls one out of her bag and gives it to me. I place it on the ground next to the cub. It sniffs the cube, then takes a bite. Soon, it devours the whole cube. The cub waddles over to me. It reaches my ankle and rubs against it. It makes a low guttural purr. I put my hand down, and it moves to my palm. I scoop it up and recognize the familiar spots. Almost exactly like her mother.

"Chiquita had a cub," I say, taking the little thing in my arms.

We decide to nurse her back to health, then release her into the woods once she's strong enough.

"Let's call her Mariela," I say, giving the cub Abuelita's name. Cami agrees.

"That's a good name, hermana."

We all walk back to la finca. Mariela takes playful nibbles of my fingertip. Her little teeth are pointy. She's a fighter. Just like her mother.

We leave the woods behind and continue down the dried-out stream toward the house. I think of our bees. A giant hornet will try to locate a honeybee colony to destroy it. But the bees will form a hive around the hornet and bring their collective temperature to 116 degrees. That's the max the bees can survive. A hornet can survive at a max of 115 degrees. One degree makes all the difference.

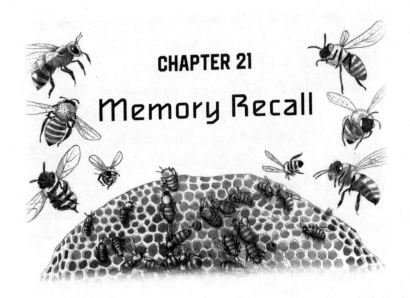

CHAPTER 21

Memory Recall

Cami and I are sitting on the porch as Arelis and Cornelius prepare to head back home. We huddle close, away from the side of the house that is still charred and burnt. It's one of the places that survived the fire.

"We want to redirect fiber-optic cables in Silo toward the Outer Valley," Arelis says, looking out to the fields that are completely ashen and still slightly smoking.

"And get the people there connected," Cornelius adds, finishing her thought.

"Come back and visit us soon," I tell her, feeling an emptiness rising in my stomach. It's the kind of feeling that comes from not wanting someone to leave, even though you know they have to. "Maybe you'll even get into bee-keeping."

"Yeah, not likely, amiga," Arelis says.

We both laugh and then say our goodbyes. We're different. That's not a bad thing. Cornelius and Cami seem to be lost in each other's eyes for a little longer than I'm comfortable watching.

"You'll see each other again," I call out.

"Yeah, don't be gross with those googly eyes, Stink Face. You look like a sad animal left outside in the cold rain."

"Okay, you two," Cami says. "Take it down a notch. We haven't seen each other in a really long time."

"It won't be so long next time," Cornelius says.

Arelis and I look at each other and cry out at the same time, "Awwww!"

Cornelius shakes his head.

"Ignore them," Cami says.

They leave, and I get that little sinking feeling of saying goodbye and wishing tomorrow were already here so we could see each other again.

It's been months since Hortensia and Mayor Blackburn were freed (at my request) and decided to leave the Valley. Nobody knows where they are or if they've survived outside the Valley. They're completely off the grid.

My wrist has healed. La finca is still only half rebuilt. It will take time. We transferred bees to a new hive box. They've already begun to forage from nectar and pollen in our fields. The strawberries are already starting to grow. They're small, dark red, sweet, and absolutely delicious.

The System has been resurrected after we salvaged its best parts, but it's under new management. Arelis is operating most of it through the Free Network now. We gathered the programmers working for the mayor and gave them new jobs: going across the Valley telling people how to access the System without paywalls. TIE classes are free.

The Méndez girls were the first to sign up for *all* the classes. Andrés is their teacher. That guy knows *everything* about tech. The girls and a group of their friends have asked for sign language lessons as well. They all want to speak like he does. Chat rooms are free. Rentals are free. Privacy is whenever anyone wants it.

We're making plans to grow more hives. More colonies. Once people learn how to tend to them, we plan to expand the colony. Abuelita's book shows us how. She thought of everything. We plan on using Valle to help transfer hive boxes when we need to extract honey. She still has only one arm but does a pretty good job. Cami still thinks we should get an upgrade.

Now *she's* the one asking for upgrades.

I let the breeze from the evening air tickle my feet. I've been walking around barefoot lately. I like the feeling of wet grass on my feet after the water sprays it.

We sit quietly on the porch. Valle hovers idly on the grass below.

I look around our home. I used to get annoyed at my sister for always putting her attention to preserving this old farm. I thought, how could she care about preserving a place that was a constant reminder of everything that went wrong?

But it was never about what was wrong. It was about what we needed to fix to make things right. The past can teach us a lot about what we decide to do with our present. Abuelita would have liked that.

The night bird starts its evening song. Mariela is cuddled at my feet. She'll soon be big enough to venture off on her own. I look at my sister. We look alike. But we're different. Like two halves that were better when they came together and became whole. With a little help from Mamá and Abuelita—our original queen bee.

CHAPTER 22

Aftermath

"Maybe I'll start an agricultural school?" Cami says, kicking around the idea. "Teach kids about bees?"

"That would be cool," I say.

"You could go back to school. Finish that neurolink degree you always wanted. No scholarships to worry about. Just free education."

"I don't know if I want that anymore," I tell her honestly. "Maybe we should travel outside of the Valley? Look for people who were unjustly exiled. Help them out. If there are any."

"Mamá always talked about that," she says, looking past the fields toward the setting sky. "Always wanted to 'find the survivors.'"

"You miss them, huh?"

Cami nods. I see her watching the sky. "Yeah," she says.

We sit in the quiet evening for a while. I drift in and out of thought.

Valle starts beeping.

"What is it, Valle?"

She turns. Her screen lights up.

"What is she saying?" Cami inspects the messages scrolling across Valle's screen.

"I can't . . . Slow down, Valle! You're going too fast!"

Valle keeps scrolling in broken messages. I stand and try to read the screen. I can't read what she's trying to report.

"I told you that thing has been busted for months," Cami says, tapping Valle on the head.

"She's not busted; she's trying to communicate something—"

I freeze.

"What is it?"

I don't say anything.

"What are you reading?" Cami continues.

"It says . . ." I look carefully at the message. "'Freedom.'"

"What?" Cami says, examining. "It's probably some residual glitch from when it was connected to Hortensia. Power it down, then reboot."

Valle continues to flash.

"Power it down, Yoly! It looks like it's going to blow up!"

Valle shakes; then her arm circles around. Maybe Cami's right. I need to power her down. I reach around her back to reboot her processor.

Another message flashes across her face.

"What the—"

"What is it?" Cami can't read what it says.

Valle's screen frantically runs codes across her face screen.

"That thing has gone off-grid, Yoly. Power it down."

"It says it's Mamá," I say quietly.

"What? What are you talking about?"

Valle keeps running messages across her screen.

"It's her," I say, looking carefully. "She's trying to tell us something."

Cami tells me not to listen. She says Valle is broken. But the messages keep flashing. Like Valle is fighting with herself. Or there are two things fighting for her control. Cami tries to move me out of the way, but I hold my ground. I need to see what Valle is trying to say.

"¡Mi'jas!" I hear through Valle's speakers. Cami steps back. My heart races.

"¡Vienen en camino!" Mamá calls through the speakers again.

"What? Who is coming?" I cry out, but I get no response.

I look to Cami. My mouth goes dry.

A message pings on my V-probe. Then one pings on Cami's. I pick it up off the porch bench and look at the screen flashing.

"The System," I tell Cami, barely able to speak.

Cami picks up her own V-probe and looks at it. She sees the same message I do.

Valle shuts down and goes idle again. Cami doesn't speak. Every part of me shakes.

Mamá.

She sent a warning.

She's alive.

She says it's coming.

Valle's screen glitches again. I look at her, then back at my V-probe. Cami does the same. We both read the same thing—it's the same message broadcasting across the entire Valley:

Freedom has a price. Prepare to pay.

<VOz Command Function . . . >

~~THE SCOURGE~~

REPROGRAM (CTRL function ARE122107&
YOLA012108*0110001)
New Program Title . . .

UNDERSTANDING BEES:
Based on Dr. Mariela Cicerón's *Colony Collapse Disorder:*
A Case for the Last Bees

REPROGRAM FUNCTIONABILITY: <VOz+command=
ARE122107&YOLA012108*ENTER>

<VOz configuring . . . >

Hello, and greetings! Welcome to *Understanding Bees*, an information guide based on the seminal work of the late Dr. Mariela Cicerón's *Colony Collapse Disorder: A Case for the Last Bees* with Editorial and Programming Additions by Yolanda Cicerón and Arelis Rivera.

Below, you will find a useful guide on information about bees and the importance they have for earth's crops and sustainability. Use your V-probe, biological, or alternate seeing or hearing organ to scroll down to read.

Thank you and have a wonderful day!

General Information and Classification

The most common sort of bee is the honeybee (genus *Apis*), particularly the western honeybee (*Apis mellifera*), which was the most cultivated and recognizable type of bee in the last century, and the bumblebee (genus *Bombus*). Honeybees are best known for their crucial role in pollination that is important both ecologically and commercially. They alone have been responsible for the pollination of 80 percent of all human cultivated crops, including more than a hundred food crops, medicinal plants, and food for livestock. All these crops are essential for human survival as well as human economic sustainability.

Apis mellifera and *Apis cerana* are the primary types of domesticated bees and are the main ones used in apiculture, or beekeeping, which is the cultivation of bees by humans primarily for the harvesting of honey.

Bee Biology and Behavior

Bees have three distinct body regions: the head, the thorax, and the abdomen. They have six legs and a pair of wings with a slight triangular shape, all of which sprout from the thorax. They also have compound eyes, characterized by the clustering of thousands of ommatidia (simple eyes) to allow the bee to see in many different directions at once and detect color and motion swiftly and clearly.

Generally, honeybees are reddish or brown with black bands and golden-yellow rings on their abdomens. They have little hairs on the thorax, and their legs are mostly dark brown or black, with a pollen basket on their hind legs. On their hind legs, female bees have a region of dense hairs used for collecting pollen, and a stinger at the end of their abdomens.

The Three Castes of Bees

Bees are divided into three castes: worker, drone, and queen.

Worker Bees

Worker bees make up most of the population within the hive and are the most important bee caste in the colony. Worker bees, which are the smallest bees, spend the whole of their five weeks of life working for the survival of the colony.

After a worker bee ages out of her larval stage, her first job is to clean the cells of the honeycomb to prepare it for new eggs or honey.

Once worker bees become a little older, they become babysitters, in charge of feeding and caring for newly hatched larvae. Juveniles are also tasked with attending the queen bee: cleaning her, feeding her, and removing her waste.

When worker bees are older, they are given the job of creating honey from the nectar the field bees collect, as well as guarding the hive, protecting its entrance, and challenging anything that tries to enter and does not belong.

The last stage for worker bees is when they graduate to field bees and leave the hive for the first time, tasked with the collection of nectar and pollen. Field bees also memorize the area surrounding the hive and the landing spots in order to remember how to get home.

Drone Bees

Drones are male bees whose purpose is to mate with the queen bee. A colony raises many more drones than are needed, as only a few will mate with a queen. In the fall, worker bees force the other drones out of the hive to starve. Drones are bigger than workers and have larger eyes.

Queen Bees

Each bee colony has one queen, whose only job is to lay eggs. Egg laying begins after she has mated with drones in the first few weeks of her adult life. The queen bee is the largest bee in the colony and her life span is about two to five years. A queen can lay from fifteen hundred to two thousand eggs in a day, although some days she will lay none.

What Bees Eat

Bees primarily eat nectar and pollen that are brought back to the hives by the field bees for the entire colony. Field bees use their tongues to suck up nectar that is stored in the anterior section of the digestive tract, called honey sacs. They collect pollen by grooming it off their bodies and onto special structures on their hind legs called pollen baskets. Returning foragers transfer the nectar they have collected to younger worker bees that in turn feed other members of the hive or process the nectar into honey. It is this honey-hoarding behavior of honeybees that humans have come to exploit for our sweet tooths. Young worker bees eat pollen and nectar and secrete food materials called "royal jelly" and "worker jelly" from glands in their heads. This material is fed to young larvae, and the type they get determines if they will be queens or workers.

How Bees Communicate

Honeybees communicate with chemical signals that are mostly centered on scent and taste. Each hive has a unique chemical signature that the colony members use to recognize each other and detect bees from other colonies.

When bees sting something, they send out alarm pheromones that alert the rest of the hive to the threat.

When foraging, bees use scent to detect suitable food sources and can communicate this to other bees, as some of the scent of the flowers is on the body of the foragers after they return to the hive. Their compound eyes can see ultraviolet light, which allows them to locate the sun and certain marks on flowers, and polarized light, which allows them to navigate.

Dancing

Bees also dance to communicate. Workers and queens can hear the vibrations of these dances. Round dances indicate food within about fifty-five yards of the hive and "waggle dances" indicate the direction and distance of food farther away, using the position of the sun to communicate direction and the bees' memory of the way back to the hive to communicate distance.

Defense

Bees defend themselves primarily by way of a venomous sting. The worker bees' stingers have barbs on them that stick in the victim's skin and break off upon use, rupturing the workers' abdomens and effectively killing them after a stinging. A worker will sacrifice herself for the overall protection of the colony. Queen bees' stingers do not have these barbs, so they can sting as many times as they want. Honeybees are docile and will not sting humans or animals attempting to move them or harvest honey unless a direct threat to the brood, the queen, the structural integrity of the hive, or their lives is detected. Since stinging only works on fleshy animals, Asian bees defend themselves against other insects mostly by "balling," in which a mass of workers surround the insect and then vibrate their muscles to generate body heat hot enough to kill it. The European honeybee does not have this heat-balling behavior.

Honeybee Habitats

Honeybees live in places with an abundant supply of suitable flowering plants—primarily meadows, open wooded areas, and gardens—but will live anywhere if there is sufficient water, food, and shelter. In order to survive, bees build enclosed nests called hives in which to house their colonies, raise their young, and produce and store their surplus food (honey). In the wild, bees choose caves, rock cavities, and hollow trees as nesting sites, and in warmer climates, they sometimes build exposed hanging hives.

A single bee colony can house anywhere from ten thousand to eighty thousand bees.

Honey Production

Honey is a food that results from the bees collecting nectar from flowers in their honey sacs and then processing the nectar within the hive by adding enzymes and reducing the water content below 18 percent. To create about a pound of honey, honeybees fly an average total of fifty-five thousand miles, visiting up to two million flowers collectively. A worker bee will look for blooms around a four-mile radius from the hive, visiting about a hundred of them per foraging trip. In order to make honey, field bees come back to the hive with nectar from flowers and mix it with an enzyme (just known as the "bee enzyme") in their mouths. The nectar is regurgitated to the hive bees, who then ingest it, transfer it to their honey sacs, mix it with more enzyme, and regurgitate it again to another bee. This process continues for as long as twenty minutes until the honey is ready to put into the honeycomb cells. Then, as the honey is still wet, the bees fan their wings over it, drying it up a bit. Then, the bees will cap the cells with a thin layer of wax and then the honey will be ready for consumption.

The Apiculturist's Job

The way that beekeepers harvest honey has seldom changed throughout the ages. Smoke is still the most effective at clouding the bees' pheromone receptors and thus calming them. Really, the smoke is tricking them into thinking nothing wrong is happening while the comb is removed from their hive. Another theory is that the smoke mimics a wildfire, and the bees drink up honey in advance of an anticipated departure to escape the fire: with a full belly the bees are not aggressive. In any case, smoke does calm the bees. After smoking out a hive, beekeepers don protective gear (which now consists of a full-body suit with a hat enshrouded with a veil) and will use a sharp device to cut off sections of comb, which, of course, are replete with honey.

Population Decline Last Century

In the twenty-first century, both climate change and the intensive use of pesticides have caused . . .

<VOz activation terminated>

<unknown source detected>

Acknowledgments

First, my thanks to Mother Nature, who is begging for us to listen and care for the Earth and its creatures (yes, including ourselves). Second, to all the young activists out there forcing us to PAY ATTENTION to climate change—I thank you and I'm listening. Third, to the bees. Don't swat them; they're helping us out.

My immense gratitude to my editor, Carolina Ortìz, for her amazing insight and spirit—GRACIAS! The team at Harper— Las Hermanas Cicerón are in your extremely capable hands, and I thank you for taking care of them. My thanks to Carlos Vélez Aguilera for his incredible illustrations and stunning cover! It really is a dope cover, isn't it? To my friend and the greatest agent in the world, Jess Regel. There's simply nobody better. To my research assistant, Sophie Tirado, thank you for aggregating pages and pages of source material and helping me sift through the mountains of research data I had to do for this story.

Research is a key to this game, and I want to give my proper shouts. To Dr. Michael Pirson at Fordham University, thank you for your insight and time. Dr. Pirson is a scholar of humanistic management, and our conversation on human dignity and society was essential to me in building the world of this novel. To Dr. Jeff Pettis, thank you for fact-checking my research on bees and their functions! To the bee farms across southeastern Vermont and South Florida with whom I spent a great deal of time learning (and getting stung more times than I care to admit). Because of local farms, I was able to understand the function of bees and their effects on the environment and our daily lives. Buy and support local farms as much as possible. A special shout-out to Marcie Davis at Bee My Honey, a wonderful apiary in Miami with incredible educational resources. Check them out at www.beemyhoney.buzz. They're awesome. I have more research thanks than these pages allow, so let me just say—read the articles, trust the work scientists are doing, climate change is real, bees aren't bad, don't use chemicals that mess with nature.

Lastly, to my beloved family—they go on research trips with me, they take pictures, they record, they support my work with all the love in their hearts. Family is everything; whatever that looks like to you, I hope you have it and cherish it. I know I do.

Gracias,

Pablo